*"Why D[...]*
*Here into t[...]*

"Not to see you, if [...] you mean,"
she retorted, her voice husky.

"It is what I mean." His voice was as uneven
as her own. "But you're lying, Ashleigh
Stevens. You hoped I'd be here. Those
devastating black eyes of yours were sending
me invitations—burning holes in me all
through dinner. It was all I could do not to
make a grab at you—and you knew it."

"I . . . I didn't," she whispered. "I don't
know what you're talking about. Maybe I'm
getting a fever too . . ."

"Maybe we both are," he muttered. And then
he was kissing her hungrily.

---

## DOROTHY CORK

was born in Australia and has lived there most
of her life. Her many readers may well have
guessed this, as her entertaining novels are
frequently set in her native land. Not that she
limits herself to this region. She is an enthusiastic and perceptive traveler. Her wholehearted
enjoyment of life is reflected in her lively romances.

Dear Reader:

I'd like to take this opportunity to thank you for all your support and encouragement of Silhouette Romances.

Many of you write in regularly, telling us what you like best about Silhouette, which authors are your favorites. This is a tremendous help to us as we strive to publish the best contemporary romances possible.

All the romances from Silhouette Books are for you, so enjoy this book and the many stories to come.

Karen Solem
Editor-in-Chief
Silhouette Books

# DOROTHY CORK
# Chosen Wife

*Silhouette* *Romance*

Published by Silhouette Books New York

America's Publisher of Contemporary Romance

SILHOUETTE BOOKS, a Division of Simon & Schuster, Inc.
1230 Avenue of the Americas, New York, N.Y. 10020

Distributed by Pocket Books

ISBN: 0-671-57304-7

First Silhouette Books printing July, 1984

10 9 8 7 6 5 4 3 2 1

Map by Ray Lundgren

America's Publisher of Contemporary Romance

Printed in the U.S.A.

**Books by Dorothy Cork**

Silhouette Romance

*Secret Marriage* #77
*By Honour Bound* #103
*Reluctant Deceiver* #148
*No More Regrets* #188
*Island Spell* #219
*Outback Dreaming* #238
*The Man From the Past* #286
*Chosen Wife* #304

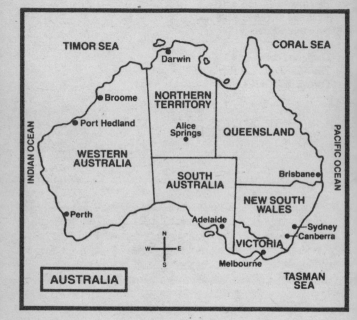

# Chapter One

So this was romantic Broome, the Port of Pearls.

Ashleigh moved into the shade of a coconut palm and narrowed her dark eyes as she studied the local map she'd just bought at a tiny store. She was itching to explore, but it soon became obvious that without a car she wasn't going to see very much, if anything. Gantheaume Point and the dinosaur's footprints, Cable Beach with its twenty-two kilometres of white sand— they were miles away. So was the cemetery, where all those pearl-divers from the past were buried and Shinto headstones marked the graves of the Japanese.

She just wasn't going to see a thing, she thought gloomily, and absent-mindedly pushed her dark hair behind her ears. She wasn't even going to catch sight of a single cultured pearl. They were leaving early in the morning and she felt a burning sense of frustration, of irritation with Don, who was in such a damned *hurry* to get to Darwin. She'd been naive enough to think they'd take their time, do some sight-seeing; but from the

7

moment they left Perth Don had driven like a bat out of
hell and hadn't even let either Ashleigh or Laura take a
turn at the wheel—not even for five minutes.

"You don't need to worry about my stamina, if that's
what's on your mind, Leigh," he'd said yesterday when
she'd tried to persuade him to let her drive and give him
a break. "I can go without sleep for twenty-four hours
and more if I have to. Besides, I don't trust women
drivers."

Ashleigh had grimaced and glanced over her shoulder to see how Laura in the back seat had taken that
remark, expecting they'd exchange rueful looks, or
something like that. But Laura had her eyes closed and
Ashleigh turned back again and looked at Don through
her lashes. She was beginning to discover, rather
disturbingly, that she didn't know him as well as she'd
imagined. He was certainly tough—which was one of
the things she'd admired in him. He was rugged,
auburn-haired, bearded, tall and sinewy. Everyone
liked Don, except Aunt Esme, who insisted that a man
who switched jobs—and not even the right sort of jobs
at that—as frequently as Don did was *not* the right sort
of man for Ashleigh Stevens. He wasn't in the least like
the men Aunt Esme and Uncle Walter were always
trying to marry her off to. If Aunt Esme had even
dreamed that Laura had a brother who was a break-
away, she'd have taken firm steps to see that Ashleigh
didn't visit the Harrises when he was around. Ashleigh
might think it was thrilling that he'd once worked for an
outfit that ran camel safaris in the desert of Central
Australia, but Esme was not impressed.

Nor was Esme impressed by the fact that Don was
about to settle down. He was buying out Jabiru Safari
Tours in Darwin and expected to take over completely
as soon as he'd learned the ropes from the present
owner. A very doubtful venture, Esme said, and Wal-

ter agreed. Besides, who'd ever want to live in Darwin? they asked.

Privately, Ashleigh thought *she* might—though she'd never been there. In fact, she'd never been north of Capricorn. Once she'd come close to it when she'd persuaded Milton Wade, a geologist with her Uncle Walter's mining company, to take her with him on a brief air journey north—brief in that he was to return to Perth the same day. But Esme had got wind of it and asked Walter to put a stop to it. Which he did, reminding Ashleigh that her parents had been killed in a small-plane crash, and that he and Esme didn't want her taking risks. But Ashleigh suspected it was mainly because they didn't want her getting involved with Milton—who was *not* on her aunt's list of men who were eligible. She'd seen practically nothing of Milton since, not surprisingly, as he valued his job with the company.

However, Ashleigh was north of Capricorn now, and she intended to stay here a long while—maybe forever. She was supposed to be going home in three weeks' time when Laura's annual holiday would be finished, but she wasn't going. It had been Don's idea that the two girls should go to Darwin with him, and Ashleigh had accepted the invitation eagerly and defiantly. She knew that Don was attracted to her and thought it would be marvellous to be away from the eagle eye of her aunt, able to let go and discover for herself just how she felt about him, without someone jumping on her back all the time.

There'd been a tremendous row over her going. She was nearly twenty and yet she was expected to ask permission! It was humiliating. Even worse was the fact that she'd had to resort to tears to get her own way—a thing she hadn't done in a long time. Walter had given in because he had a soft side to his nature, and Esme had said angrily that it was madness to let Ashleigh go away with a dangerous man like Don Harris. Being Laura's brother, Don almost certainly knew that Ashleigh had a very nice little inheritance coming to her when she married, and one could just imagine how much an irresponsible man like that would like to get his hands on it, Esme speculated aloud.

"But darling," Walter had said, trying to justify his weakness, "Ashleigh's not marrying Don Harris—she's not even going away with the man. She's taking a holiday with Laura, that's all. They're going with Don for the transport."

It had made Ashleigh squirm to see the quandary Walter was in and she felt worse still because of the way she was deceiving him. She hadn't the least intention of coming back to Perth, and it was because of Don, not because of Laura, that she was going. Esme, with a woman's intuition, knew better than Walter, and Ashleigh was well aware that her uncle would have gone mad if he'd known she planned to work as hostess on the safari tours and that she'd probably marry Don as well. He hadn't actually asked her yet, but she knew it was only because he wanted to make sure she'd fit in with the life he was going to live. Ashleigh knew she would fit in.

But right now, in Broome, her enthusiasm wasn't exactly what it had been. She was bothered by a few niggling little doubts. No one was perfect of course; but three whole days of his company had taught her things about Don that she hadn't known before. One thing was his prejudice against women drivers. Another was that he liked to make all the plans. He didn't bother to consult her or Laura about a single thing, and Ashleigh didn't really like to be taken charge of that way. It was too much like home. She hadn't run away from her restricted life in Perth to be kept in check by somebody else. What she wanted was freedom to be herself. She wanted excitement, adventure, the taste of real life—all the things she'd been protected from ever since her mother's elegant sister had become responsible for Ashleigh when she was nine years old.

It would be different once they reached Darwin, she assured herself. At present, Don was concerned with getting there, and of course nothing was new to him as it was to her. He'd traveled this way so many times it wasn't exciting to him.

And when she came to think of it, wasn't she free at this minute? Yet she didn't know how to use her freedom. And that was something she was going to have to work on or she'd be running back to Perth, looking for her hutch like a frightened rabbit. It was—disenchanting.

"Move," she told herself. "Use your initiative—do something resourceful."

Such as what? She hadn't a clue, and as if hoping for inspiration, she began to walk down towards the bay. The tide was halfway out and moving fast—it rose and fell about eight metres twice a day, which accounted for the staggeringly long jetty—but even so, the water looked fantastically beautiful. There was a deep indigo strip on the horizon, then an expanse of jewel green, while near the sand—*pink* sand—where a few children played, it was a clear yellowish green. Nearby, a couple of boats were stranded. "Pearling luggers!" she thought hopefully. But even if they were—so what? There was nobody about to answer any questions.

She turned away disconsolately, wishing Laura were still around. But Laura had caught some kind of a virus—which explained her apathy in the car yesterday —and they'd left her in Port Hedland with Robyn and Ted, Don's friends who'd put them up for the night. Don had friends everywhere—contacts to make as they hared across the state. Laura had said she'd fly on to Darwin when she was better and insisted that they should go on without her. Not that she'd needed to insist; Don had no intention of doing anything else but go on, though Ashleigh wanted to stay. But the very thought of that had made Laura almost burst into tears.

"No, Ashleigh. I'd never forgive myself. You go on with Don—I'm being looked after."

So they'd left at piccaninny daylight this morning, and Don had driven like a demon the whole 650 kilometres to Broome, along the newly sealed Great Northern Highway. They made a half-hour stop at the Sandfire Flat Roadhouse, for petrol and something to eat, and that was only because there was nowhere else to get it on that long stretch of pindan country.

It all seemed like a century ago, and suddenly Ashleigh decided she'd go back to the motel and ring Port Hedland to find out how Laura was. The decision on some kind of action had her almost running and she forced herself to slow down. She must be catching the rush habit from Don. Nobody hurried in Broome and anyhow, exactly where was she going in such a tear? What happened after she'd rung up about Laura? She'd look for Don, she supposed, but she didn't think he'd relent and take her sight-seeing. He'd already knocked that idea back when they'd unloaded their gear at the motel and she'd come to his door and suggested it.

"Sight-seeing? Forget it. We'll have a shower and get ourselves a drink. I don't want to go traipsing around looking at things I've seen before. I've been driving all day. All I want is to sit about and relax."

"Okay," Ashleigh had said mildly, and moved back next door to her own unit. What had happened to Don's famous energy, she'd wondered. Maybe he *had* seen everything before, but she hadn't. Nor was it her fault he'd been driving all day. . . .

She dawdled along, trying to console herself with the lovely sight of the tall coconut palms, the boabs with their weird bottle-shaped trunks, and the frangipanis that scented the air almost overpoweringly and seemed to grow in every garden—white or creamy or lusciously pink.

At the motel, she made her telephone call and was far from cheered to hear from Robyn that Laura was really sick and had been delirious. They'd had the doctor to see her, she was on antibiotics, and there was positively nothing to worry about, Robyn reported.

"Just don't expect her in Darwin too soon," Robyn said firmly. "I'm going to make sure she's really back on her feet before I let her go."

Ashleigh went to look for Don and pass on the news. It occurred to her that Walter and Esme would scream blue murder if they knew that Laura would be off the scene for a week or two and that she'd be alone with Don. Well, they weren't going to know, and what they didn't know wouldn't hurt them. After all, it wasn't as if she were doing anything she shouldn't do—like sleeping with Don. All that had happened so far was that he'd kissed her good night a couple of times. Otherwise he'd acted more like a rather bossy elder brother than anything else. Which, if she were quite honest, had rather disappointed her. She'd thought he'd be wilder, more passionate. . . .

She found her way to the big lattice-screened downstairs lounge, but he wasn't there. A sign by the stairway pointed up to the Cavern Cocktail Lounge, and outside to the swimming pool. Ashleigh frowned. She didn't fancy sitting drinking in some dim dark airless place, and if Don were there, he could have it to himself. She'd have a swim; she wished she'd thought of that before.

The garden was tropical—full of brilliant canna lilies; big, fan-shaped traveller's palms, leafy banana plants; and all kinds of shrubs with exotic flowers. A Dutchman's-pipe vine clambered over a wire trellis, its big speckled flowers looking positively artificial. Ashleigh ducked her head as she walked under a frangipani tree, picked up one of the fallen pink flowers, and sniffed at it deeply. There was a small lawn ahead of her with a sprinkler playing on it and beyond, at a table in the shade of some trees, Don was sitting, but not alone. There were two people with him—a girl with curly brown hair and huge sun-glasses and a broad-shouldered, dark-haired man whose back was towards Ashleigh.

So Don had run into friends again, she thought, and for some reason her step lightened.

"Come on and join us," Don invited as she drew near. "I was beginning to wonder if you'd stowed away on a pearling lugger."

The dark-haired man rose to his feet and turned round as he did so, his glance taking her in rapidly. He wore smart but casual white pants and a short-sleeved dark blue shirt, his hair was thick and dark, his face deeply tanned, and his eyes—they were like aquamarines. Dazzling. They made her catch her breath, they did something to her—because of the expression in them, she realised dimly, a look that said almost blatantly, "You're a woman—"

Somehow embarrassed, even shocked, she looked quickly away from him, her cheeks burning.

Don reached out and pulled her down into the chair next to his.

"This is Ashleigh Stevens." The way he said it sounded to Ashleigh as if he'd been talking about her, and she wondered fleetingly what he'd been saying. "Leigh, meet Debra Davis, an acquaintance of mine from Darwin. And Ryan Langton."

Ashleigh heard herself say hello in a voice that didn't seem to belong to her. She tried to concentrate on Debra Davis, who was leaning back and smiling at her in a friendly way, but in a split second her gaze had flown to Ryan Langton and her eyes were tangling with his. It was something she seemed helpless to resist—a physical thing, as strong as the current on the edge of rapids, which somehow was a very apt description of the way she was feeling right now.

"What can I get you to drink, Ashleigh?" His voice was pleasant with a faint Australian drawl in it, but there was something about his smile that seemed to suggest that he knew perfectly well how she was reacting to him, and she felt at an immediate disadvantage. She moistened her lips, but before she could speak, Don put his hand on her wrist and answered for her. "She'll have orange juice. Won't you, Leigh?"

She nodded and Debra laughed.

"Is that your taste, Leigh? Or is it all Don allows you? He's a bit of a chauvinist, I suspect."

A chauvinist? Was that what you'd call Don? It had never occurred to Ashleigh, and now it was Debra Davis's smile she didn't much like. It made her seem knowing, superior. She and that man probably belonged together, Ashleigh realised rather belatedly. A quick glance revealed that Debra didn't wear a ring, but that meant nothing.

Ashleigh murmured something about not liking alcohol in the heat of the day and took Debra in rapidly. Slim, self-confident, with curly light-brown hair, an even sun-tan. She wore dark beige cotton pants and a beige blouse with long sleeves and a mandarin collar—smart but practical. Her make-up looked so natural one would think she wasn't wearing any. But she was. Ashleigh, who was wearing only a touch of lip colour, knew about things like that, because Esme had insisted on sending her to a modelling school last year. Not to learn to be a model ("God forbid," her aunt had said), but to learn how to walk, how to dress, how to make the most of her appearance. . . . which at this identical moment she was definitely not doing, because she hadn't even glanced in a mirror since they'd hit Broome. She was still wearing the pale lime shorts and pink blouse she'd had on all day, and she'd pushed her dark, shining hair back behind her ears and hadn't even run a comb through it. She probably looked so immature it was a wonder a man like Ryan Langton had even glanced at her.

Anyhow, he was moving off, presumably to get her an orange juice, and she sank back in her chair, glad of what seemed oddly like a respite.

"What did you see in the town, Leigh?" Don asked.

Ashleigh blinked. She'd scarcely looked at Don since she'd sat down and now she felt a kind of surprise that he'd left it to Ryan Langton to get her drink. There were no drink waiters or waitresses buzzing around here in the garden, and it seemed that guests who didn't sit in the bar or the lounge had to look after themselves.

"Nothing much. I couldn't be bothered wandering about on my own," she said reluctantly. She felt oddly disinclined to talk. All she wanted to do was to lean back in her chair. Maybe it was just the heat, the lazy atmosphere, but she felt as if she were under the spell of a drug—or an aphrodisiac, she thought unexpectedly. Yet she hadn't the faintest idea what it would be like to be given an aphrodisiac, so what was she thinking of? "I telephoned Port Hedland just now," she said hastily. "To find out how Laura is."

"Oh, Don's poor little sister," Debra put in, with what Ashleigh thought was a heartless laugh. "And how is she?"

"Yes, how is my sister? Completely recovered?" Don was smiling too, his brownish hazel eyes bright. "I suspect she was fed up with the outback. Not so much sick as chickening out, if you ask me."

Ashleigh looked at him, puzzled. Laura was delirious; Robyn had said so. Her lips parted to protest when

Ryan Langton came back with a tall, frosty glass of orange juice and placed it on the table before her. Instead of arguing with Don, she murmured her thanks, though she didn't dare look up, and found she was wishing she'd taken out her vanity mirror and tidied herself up a little.

"Of course, you city girls from the south are soft," Debra was commenting, a note of amused patronage in her voice. From behind her sun-glasses, her glance lingered on the very slightly crumpled pale pink blouse Ashleigh was wearing, as if its very colour were an indication of softness, Ashleigh thought touchily.

"Are the girls from the north all that different?" she asked, her velvety brown eyes innocently wide. "I thought you were from Darwin. That's a city too, isn't it?"

"A city with a difference," Debra retorted. "A frontier city, a city that's pulled itself up by its shoe strings since Cyclone Tracy blew it to pieces at Christmas '74. I was there—home from school on holidays. Our house was flattened and my parents"—she flung out her hands briefly—"they went south. My mother had had enough. But *I'm* back again. I couldn't keep away. It's a place you either love or hate. You'll find out, if you get as far as that."

Oh I'll get there, Ashleigh thought. For some reason Debra's remarks made her hackles rise. She seemed intent on taking Ashleigh down a peg or two, on making out that she was inferior in some way just because she came from Perth. Ashleigh sipped her drink and said nothing. She'd get to Darwin all right, Debra would find out. And if she wanted to be subtly rude by making out that Ashleigh was an outsider, then she could have it all on her own. Ashleigh didn't care a cent what the girl thought of her.

Then, as if something forced her to do it, she looked

at Ryan Langton through her lashes. He was looking straight back at her and she flushed with a curious guiltiness.

"I take it you haven't been to Darwin before, Ashleigh," she heard him say, the remark half a question.

"No." She could hear the defensiveness in her voice, and added with forced brightness, "But there always has to be a first time, doesn't there? Is that where you're from?"

"No, I'm from the East Kimberleys. We've just been hearing that Don is taking over the Jabiru Safari Tours and that you're going to work with him." His glance flicked over her mockingly, she thought; or was it pityingly? At any rate, she didn't like it.

"It's a flourishing little business," Don said, leaning back in his chair and stroking his beard. "Do you know Len Carson? Debra knows his wife, Caryl—"

"Caryl and I were at school together," Debra put in. "We see each other now and again, and I know Len quite well. Ryan wouldn't know him—would you, Ryan? Caryl's finding it hard carrying on the hostessing now she's pregnant. She and Len are going to take up a small holding on the Ord River, near her parents' property. I believe they're both looking forward to it, though it will be a hard life in many ways. Still, they're both Territorians."

Ashleigh tried not to read any more slights or innuendoes into what Debra was saying—but of course *she* wasn't a Territorian. But then neither was Don, though no one who knew the kind of life he led could suggest *he* was soft and citified; and if he thought she could cope with the Territory, then that was good enough for her. She'd show Debra Davis, she thought.

The others were still talking, but she was listening with only half her mind. The other half was on the man sitting on her left side. Through her lashes she could see his thigh, hard and muscular-looking under the fine white cloth of his pants, and she had an almost irresistible impulse to reach out and put her hand on it. What would Don think? And what would *he* think?

At exactly that point in her reflections, Ryan reached out and flicked at her breast right at its most sensitive point. The colour rushed to her face and he said lightly, "Sorry about that. A tiny spider. Must mean money."

Ashleigh didn't know whether to believe him or not, or whether he was being impertinent. She looked away from him quickly, and to her relief, realised that the other two had missed the little bit of byplay. They were talking about the Ord, the dam, the immense amount of money spent on it, the opinion some people held that it was an enormous fiasco. But neither Don nor Debra shared that opinion. They were both convinced there was a great future for the Ord.

"I covered it in an article a few months ago," Debra said. "Or at least, when I say I covered it, I touched the surface. Actually I'm wrapped in it. You've been there, I suppose, Don?"

Sure, Don had been there. He'd been everywhere, Ashleigh caught herself thinking. She was wondering what Ryan Langton thought about the Ord irrigation scheme when Debra remarked, "You're not passing an opinion, Ryan. You do have one, I'm sure."

"Yes, I have one." He got to his feet. "But if you folks will excuse me, I'm going in to shower and change for dinner. Are you coming, Debra?"

"Right away." She got to her feet with a fluid movement that Ashleigh couldn't help but admire; at the same time Ashleigh was taking in the intimacies suggested by the way Ryan Langton had spoken, as though he and Debra shared a suite. Which they probably did, she reflected uneasily. They were mature types who could have a relationship of that kind without even thinking about it, nothing like herself and Don, in fact. . . .

"We'll see you at dinner," Debra said.

"Sure," Don nodded, and the other two smiled and disappeared.

Almost immediately, the sky began to darken. A flood of burnt orange came over it, burnishing the palm leaves, the grass, Don's face. It was . . . romantic. Ashleigh leaned back in her chair and sighed. She didn't really want to have dinner with Ryan Langton and Debra Davis, and she wished Don hadn't agreed so easily, or had at least consulted her.

"Where did you meet them?" she asked after a moment when Don had said nothing.

"Oh, I get around," he said jokingly. "Debra's a free-lance writer in Darwin—you caught on to that, didn't you?"

Ashleigh nodded, a little impatiently. It was Ryan she wanted to know about, she admitted to herself, though she wasn't going to admit it to Don.

"She did an article about the Jabiru Safari Tours for her magazine," Don went on. "Then she decided to get Caryl's angle, which eventually wasn't publishable— wouldn't have been the right sort of publicity. I happened to be around at the time, and that's how we met. I was doing a bit of research myself, finding out exactly what a hostess did on these trips, so I'd know if it was something you could cope with."

"And do you think it is?"

"We'll soon find out," Don said, and she felt vaguely infuriated. Because of course she could cope; it would have been nice to have Don at least on her side.

"And where did you meet him—Ryan Langton?" she persisted after a moment.

"Right here, this evening. Though I know his name, of course."

He paused and Ashleigh found she was counting three before she asked, "Why do you say 'of course'?"

"Because he's the boss of Crystal Downs cattle station, that's why."

Ashleigh's eyes widened with interest. So he was a cattleman! She might have guessed it. Don fiddled with his glass and as he looked at her she thought his eyes seemed slightly glazed. Too much to drink? No, that was definitely not one of his faults. He was probably overtired; well, he had only himself to blame for that, she thought a little unkindly.

"So what's he doing here?" she asked, trying to prompt him into telling her something more.

Don cocked one eyebrow. "I didn't bother to ask—it seemed too obvious. Well, Debra's a great girl. She'll have no trouble adapting to life on a cattle station."

No, of course she wouldn't, Ashleigh thought. She was from Darwin, a frontier city. She wasn't soft, she didn't wear pretty pink blouses. . . .

"You mean they're engaged?" she pressed.

"It's on the cards. I have an idea he's been married before, but if he wants kids, someone to take over from him later, then it's certainly time he looked for another wife."

Ashleigh frowned. *"Looked* for a wife? I should hate to marry a man who was *looking* for a wife. Where's he supposed to be looking? Under the bed? Behind the door? It sounds perfectly ridiculous to me." She picked up her glass; for some reason her fingers were trembling.

Don smiled wryly. "It's not all that ridiculous. In this part of the state, there isn't a girl lurking around every corner—or even under every bed. A man who lives on an isolated cattle station has to go out of his way to find himself a wife. . . . Why are you so interested, anyhow?"

"I'm not; I'm just curious," she retorted, and hastily swallowed down the rest of her drink. She was more than curious, although she didn't know why. It wasn't

as if she particularly liked the man. But whatever she
felt about him, at this minute her heart was beating a
fast tattoo, and she was glad Don couldn't see it, or
he'd be asking questions about that, too. She was
asking questions herself. She couldn't understand why
she should be so churned up over a man she wasn't
likely to set eyes on again after tonight.

She changed the subject. "Aren't you worried about
Laura, Don? She really is sick, you know. Robyn says it
will be a while before she can come on to Darwin."

"Oh Laura's okay. I half expected she'd drop out,"
Don said dismissively, and Ashleigh looked at him
reproachfully.

"You're not very sympathetic are you? Laura's been
delirious—Robyn told me so."

"Maybe," he shrugged. "But don't you know she
only agreed to come along on this trip so that you could
come? You'd never have made it otherwise, would
you?"

Ashleigh looked at him uncertainly. Had Laura been
putting on an act? Ashleigh could have sworn she was
hot, feverish. . . . As for whether or not she'd have
made it on her own—yes, she thought she would have.
She'd have told lies, she thought. Not only because of
Don, but because she'd been absolutely determined to
get away, to be independent—and because there was
something about the tropics that fascinated her.

"What do you think?" she said, jumping up from her
chair. "Anyhow, I'm going to get changed."

In the restaurant that night, they joined Debra and
Ryan at a table for four. Ashleigh had put on a pale
violet dress with a lace collar and tiny lace-trimmed
sleeves. The delicate colour and fabric complemented
her fair skin and emphasized the darkness of her eyes
and hair. It was a feminine look that she felt at home
with, and she couldn't help it if it reinforced Debra's
idea that she was soft. As for Ryan, she didn't care

what he thought of her, she told herself. Though at least this time her hair was tidy and she wasn't a crumpled mess, she mused illogically.

Debra, she discovered as she and Don went into the restaurant, hadn't bothered to change. Ryan had; he looked so unnervingly masculine in black pants and a black-and-tan striped shirt, whose open neck revealed the dark hair on his chest, that Ashleigh found her eyes drawn to him helplessly.

"Oh—pretty!" Debra exclaimed as Ashleigh took her place at the table. And that was about the only remark she addressed to her all evening.

Ashleigh didn't enjoy the meal much. How could she when Don for some reason seemed disinclined to talk and Ryan devoted all his attention to Debra? It was obvious they'd sooner have been alone, but there was not a thing Ashleigh could do about it, except try to act as though she weren't there.

The conversation was mostly about pearls, and Ashleigh gathered that Debra and Ryan had spent some time at the pearl auction. Debra had been commissioned by her magazine to cover the auction, to write additional material about the cultured pearl industry, and to interview old-timers both in Chinatown and in Broome proper.

Once more, in fact, Ashleigh was a complete outsider, and she looked with dislike at Ryan's darkly tanned face and the hard line of his wide mouth. He didn't meet her eye once over the meal, yet she had the feeling that every time she so much as glanced at him, he was aware of it and irritated. She was relieved when Don finished his coffee and got to his feet.

"Early to bed for us," he said, reaching out a hand to her. "We're moving off at seven sharp in the morning."

He put his arm possessively around her shoulder and she murmured a subdued good night and was disconcerted when Ryan got up from the table and offered his hand. She took it. He smiled down at her, his eyes narrowed, with that expression in them that she'd caught there before—that awareness of her as a woman. Something crazy seemed to happen inside of her. Her heart began to pound; she dropped his hand as though it had burned her. As she moved off with Don, her limbs were trembling.

Don took her arm as they went down the stairs and pulled her close to him as they walked through the lattice-walled lounge towards the path that led to the units. He hadn't held her that way before and she was suddenly nervous, because this was their first night alone—the first night she hadn't shared a room with Laura. . . . Outside her unit he waited while she unlocked the door, then stepped inside after her while she flicked on the light.

"Looks comfortable, doesn't it?" he said. Her eyes went to the bed—a double one. Was that what he meant?

"Yes," she agreed a little uncertainly. Her thoughts went fleetingly to Debra and Ryan, and she knew quite positively that things wouldn't be like this between them. Debra wouldn't be nervous. . . .

Ashleigh could see their two reflections in the big wall mirror across the room: Don in cream shirt and fawn shorts, long socks, and navy blue tie, herself looking fragile, she supposed wryly, in the violet dress, her cheeks faintly flushed, her eyes very dark. His auburn hair and auburn beard glowed like copper, and their images merged as he put his arms around her and drew her to him.

"Good night, Leigh."

He kissed her—a long kiss, his grip on her firm, his body pressed to hers. It was the first time he'd kissed her this way, and Ashleigh closed her eyes and kissed him back, and waited for fires to run along her veins. But they didn't. She felt bitterly disappointed. No fires, no thrill, no chemistry. Why not? Because she was tired after the long drive today? That must be it, she decided. He began kissing her again and she wished he'd let her go. She had an awful suspicion he was going to suggest they should spend the night together. And that was something she definitely wasn't ready for—not yet.

But to her infinite relief, she didn't have to suffer the embarrassment of having to tell him so. A moment later, he was perfectly satisfied to let her go and murmur reluctantly, "We'd better get some sleep. I'm damned tired, so I know you must be. You'll be okay on your own?"

Oh yes, she'd be okay on her own, and she nodded fervently.

"Of course," she said.

Another brief kiss, and then he slid his fingers down her bare arm. "I'll give you a call in the morning. I've arranged an early breakfast for us in the restaurant. . . . Sleep well."

She nodded again and he went. She stood where she was and drew a deep breath. His kisses hadn't stirred her, but he hadn't seemed to notice. In which case, what had it all been about?

He'd shut the door behind him, and she crossed the room and took her pyjamas from the suitcase that lay open on the luggage stand. Maybe he was tender and considerate, she thought, but he certainly wasn't passionate. Unless, like her, he was tired. . . . So what, anyhow? Did it really matter? Not unless *she* was passionate, she decided. And to date, she hadn't noticed any signs that her feelings were likely to run away with her. It could be they were well matched. Esme needn't have worried, she thought with a wry smile. So far, Don hadn't proved to be exactly dangerous.

She wandered about the room for a few minutes, but

didn't undress. She felt too unsettled. For some reason, her thoughts had strayed again to Ryan Langton sitting upstairs in the restaurant with Debra, their heads close together as they talked about pearls. By this time they might be somewhere else and talking about something far more personal—or not talking at all. *He* was a passionate man. How did she know that? She had no idea. She just knew. Maybe from that look in his eyes.

Her feeling of tiredness seemed to have deserted her, and a minute later, she was outside. The night air was full of flower scents and she made her way into the garden and found the little lawn, wet under her thin-soled shoes from the soaking it had been given earlier. There was no moon, and the sky was like a great black velvet emptiness with stars so bright they looked three-dimensional. They looked as if you could reach out and close your hand around them. A fistful of stars. . . . She stretched out her hand, her fingers curving. There was still magic in the world, in spite of science.

# Chapter Two

"Reaching for the stars? Or just striking attitudes?" a smooth, low voice said. It was Ryan Langton. It seemed curiously inevitable that he should be here. Ashleigh felt a shiver run through her as he moved in the shadow of the trees. A cigarette glowed briefly, then disappeared as he dropped it and ground it out.

"Neither. I couldn't sleep," she said. Somehow it sounded like a confession and she was furious with herself.

"Couldn't sleep? Don't tell me you go to bed in that expensive-looking mauve silk thing," he said mockingly. He'd come silently nearer and stood looking down at her.

"No, but I don't prowl around the garden in my pyjamas, either," she retorted, unevenly. He was so close she could feel the warmth vibrating from his body, smell the subtle body cologne he used. If she took a deep breath, she'd be touching him. "I thought you were engaged in a dialogue on the pearling industry, anyhow.''

"Anyhow?" he repeated, his dark eyebrows arching.

She didn't have to ask what he meant. She'd sounded exactly as if she were protesting that she hadn't come out here to look for him—which made it seem as if she had. . . .

"Debra had an after-dinner appointment with a pearl buyer," he said. "I thought it best to let her have the field to herself."

"I'm sure you could have made a valuable contribution," she said, remembering burningly how he'd ignored her at the dinner table. "You seem to know everything there is to know about cultured pearls. I'm afraid it's no use talking to me about them—I know nothing."

"I haven't the slightest desire to talk to you about pearls, Ashleigh," he said. Then asked abruptly, "Where's your boyfriend?"

"He's—he's gone to bed."

"Not waiting for you?"

"No." She wondered if he really meant what she thought he meant. She could see the dark sheen of his hair in the starlight and she had a strange desire to reach out and touch it.

"You know why, I suppose?"

Because he—Don—wasn't the passionate type, she thought inanely. That's why he wasn't waiting for her. . . . "I don't know what you mean," she said distantly, wishing she wasn't so disturbed by his nearness, the maleness of him.

"I mean he's sickening for something," he said abruptly. "Didn't his sister get left behind in Port Hedland with some sort of virus?"

"Yes. But there's nothing wrong with Don."

"Nothing wrong with him? You mean you didn't

notice that glazed look about his eyes? Or that it was all he could do to sit upright through dinner? If you have any sense, you'll keep your distance from him. Though I suppose it's too late for that," he added, and she blushed to the roots of her hair.

"I don't need advice like that," she said stiffly. "I don't know what sort of opinion you have of me, Mr. Langton, but—"

"We won't go into my opinion of you. It's hardly relevant. I'm merely being realistic, Miss Stevens. Kissing's no crime and of course you've been kissed good night. But just lay off it for awhile and give yourself a chance. You could find it worse than a nuisance if you went down with 'flu in the Kimberleys and had to be carted off to hospital. . . . Do you have separate rooms, or are you sharing your quarters?"

Ashleigh gasped. "We're not sleeping together," she exclaimed her voice low and vehement.

"I'm glad to hear it." As he spoke, he'd taken her wrist between his fingers and she felt fire run up her arm and her knees grow weak. Was he taking her pulse or—

"You go in to bed and take some aspirin," he said. "Get yourself a good sleep. Remember, you're leaving early in the morning."

As if she was likely to forget!

"We won't be doing that if Don's sick," she said perversely. The touch of his fingers on her wrist was driving her mad and suddenly she knew just what she wanted—and couldn't believe it of herself.

"Oh, I think you will," he said, his voice soft, his fingers twining in hers now. "If I were Don I'd do exactly what he's planning to do—leave for Darwin at first light—press on."

"But—but why?" she asked, scarcely able to breathe.

"Why do you think?" With a sudden rough movement, he pulled her against him so her body was in direct communication with his from the points of her breasts to the top of her thighs. "Why did you come out here into the garden tonight?"

Oh, she knew why she'd come—now. But she hadn't known before. She couldn't possibly have. "Not to see you, if that's what you mean," she retorted, her voice husky.

"It is what I mean." His voice was as uneven as her own. "But you're lying, Ashleigh Stevens. You hoped I'd be here, didn't you? Those devastating black eyes of yours were sending me invitations, burning holes in me all through dinner. It was all I could do not to make a grab at you, and you knew it."

"I—I didn't," she whispered, her head whirling. "I don't know what you're talking about. Maybe I'm getting a fever too—"

"Maybe we both are," he muttered. And then he was kissing her dementedly, hungrily. She could feel the heat of his body almost as though it were on her bare flesh. A fire seemed to run between them and her pulses drummed in her ears as she wound her arms around his neck and responded to his kisses with a knowledge she didn't even know she possessed. She could feel his desire mounting as she twisted in his arms, not in an effort to get away, but because she wanted to be closer to him—closer than this. Her hand went inside his shirt and found flesh that was hot and smooth and living, and she heard herself moan softly.

"That's enough, Ashleigh Stevens," he said, his voice scarcely audible. He took hold of her hand quite violently and removed it from his flesh. Both of them were panting slightly and Ashleigh felt a terrible weakness all through her.

"Why?" she whispered. She wanted to lean her head against his breast, she wanted everything. She was burning with desire. She, who'd thought she wasn't a passionate girl.

"No," he said, as if she'd made some completely explicit request. "You're going to do what I said—run off to bed and take some aspirin. And I'm going to walk along by the bay and pick Debra up," he added deliberately.

Debra. Of course. It was like a dash of icy water in her face, and she was suddenly desperately ashamed of the impassioned way she'd behaved. What on earth had got into her? It stunned her that she could have lost control of herself so completely with the very first man she'd met since she'd left the nest. The ludicrous thought flashed into her head that this man would pass every one of her Aunt Esme's tests. There were men who were acceptable and men who weren't, and it had taken her no time at all to be able to classify them herself, according to her aunt's standards. Ryan Langton would pass with flying colours, though of course she would never be presenting him to Esme. . . .

Meanwhile, they were strolling back through the garden towards the motel units. Without being aware of what she was doing, she took hold of his arm and felt his muscles stiffen, felt too a thrill run through her that was positively frightening. How could it possibly be that such a small thing as touching his arm could have such volcanic results?

He didn't take her as far as the door of her suite. Which was just as well, she thought. Because if he'd stepped inside for a minute, it wouldn't have been like that harmless interlude with Don. . . .

As they reached the lighted path, he said a curt good night, released his arm from her clinging fingers, and left her.

In the warm, empty room she stood shivering, her whole body tingling with the kind of desires she'd never experienced before, the kind of feelings she'd expected

Don to arouse in her. And because he hadn't—yes, that was it, she decided. She'd been compensating. It was as simple as that.

Anyhow, Ryan Langton was too mature for her. She was glad they were leaving in the morning. Unless of course Don was too ill and they had to stay on.

Without being aware of what she was doing, she'd got into her pyjamas and into bed, where she lay under the sheet in the darkness and tried not to think of that man.

The boss of Crystal Downs cattle station. A man in his thirties, who'd been married before and had reached the stage where he needed to marry again. Or so Don had said. But what did Don know about it? Oh God—the questions she wished she'd asked Ryan Langton now! They'd have made Esme look like a novice as an inquisitor. Yet questions weren't going to rid her of her restlessness, or ease the painful longings she had that were more than half physical, and of which she was vaguely ashamed. She tried to persuade herself that when she woke in the morning she'd laugh at herself. But right now morning seemed a long way off.

She slept eventually, and at dawn, the telephone on the bedside table rang. It was Don waking her, and she got out of bed at once, her mind taking note of the fact that there was apparently nothing wrong with Don, so Ryan Langton had been wrong. Ashleigh wasn't ready to think about Ryan coolly and rationally yet. She pushed him to the back of her mind, scrambled into her pants and shirt, bundled her things into her suitcase, and went up to the restaurant to join Don for breakfast.

"Feeling okay?" he asked, already finishing his toast and marmalade.

She nodded. "Are you?"

"Great," he said. "I needed that sleep . . . I'll leave you to finish your brekkie while I load the car. Let me have your key, will you?"

Ashleigh didn't hurry. Deep inside, she was hoping she'd catch another glimpse of Ryan Langton. Though why she should imagine he'd get out of his bed (probably a bed he was sharing with Debra Davis, she reminded herself) merely for a last look at her, she simply didn't know.

She went back to her room at last to pick up her toothbrush and a few odds and ends, stuff them into the hold-all she'd brought, and hurry into the fresh early morning to the car where Don was waiting.

Good bye to Broome, she thought as they drove through the streets. She'd seen precious little of it and she didn't have the energy or the heart to suggest Don should drive her out for a look at Gantheaume Point or Cable Beach. She'd thought of Broome as a romantic place, but now she reminded herself of the merciless cyclones, the destruction of pearling luggers, the number of divers of many different nations who'd lost their lives diving for pearl shells. An industry that was now barely alive—killed by the advent of the plastic button! It was . . . tawdry. And so was her own spasm of romanticism and passion.

One thing she'd remember about Broome forever though was that it had housed at least one very sexually potent male, who'd taught her something about herself that she'd really rather not have learned from him.

She glanced at Don, ashamed of the thoughts she was having. He'd be stunned if he knew what was going on in her mind. But he didn't look as if he were even aware of her. He was frowning slightly as he groped in the glove box for his sun-glasses, and he put them on without speaking to her.

The morning developed into the same mad race as the last three days. There was a map, but Ashleigh soon lost track of where they were, because Don didn't follow the main road system. They were heading towards Derby, but before they reached it, he turned the car onto the road to Gibb River, sealed for perhaps seventy kilometres and after that unsealed across the King Leopold Range. Ashleigh was lost in no time and put the map away. The going was rough and dusty and for once she was thankful she wasn't expected to take the wheel.

When they stopped for lunch by a billabong where paper-barks hung over the water and small brightly coloured birds darted about in search of insects, she looked at Don in slight alarm. His face was flushed and his eyes were bright. Glazed, Ryan had said. He seemed irritable, too, as she set out the lunch he'd had packed for them at the motel.

"Are you all right, Don? I hope you're not getting that virus that Laura had."

"What virus?" He looked back at her coldly. "I told you, Laura's playing possum. She knew I intended to come this way and she chickened out. I'm okay. I never get sick."

Ashleigh bit into a sandwich. "Where are we staying tonight?" she asked mildly, deciding it was no use arguing with him. "Will we get as far as Kununurra?"

"No, we won't." Don looked at her hopelessly. "Use your head, Leigh. That would be pushing it a bit too hard in this kind of country. Besides, I have some friends on a cattle station between here and Kununurra. I want to call in on them and we'll stay there."

Ashleigh widened her eyes. "That sounds interesting! It must be exciting to live on a cattle station," she enthused.

"About as exciting as it is for a fly to fall into a jug of milk," Don said flatly. "All a girl like you would want is out. Darwin will be more to your taste. So don't go getting any other ideas into your head."

Any other ideas? Was that by any chance a crack at her for her interest in Ryan Langton? But all she'd done was ask Don a few questions. Or had her interest showed some other way? Oh God, she hoped not. Yet Ryan had said that if he were Don, he'd press on today. And they were certainly pressing on.

She finished her sandwich, poured out two mugs of tea from the big thermos they'd brought, and then began packing up. She wondered where Ryan's cattle station, Crystal Downs, was, but she wasn't going to ask. She wasn't going to encourage herself to think about Ryan Langton. She was going to forget him as completely as he had undoubtedly forgotten her. . . .

They pressed on again. The road grew rougher and dustier, running along by a flat-topped range covered with scrub and tufts of spiky spinifex grass. Masses of small starry pink flowers grew along the track and amongst the trees Ashleigh caught the chrome yellow gleam of wattles and the fire red of grevilleas. The range petered out and they passed a turkey nest tank and a windmill, where a narrow road meandered off, presumably to some station, though there was no gate, no sign. However did you tell where you were in this sort of country? she wondered.

She was about to ask Don when, unexpectedly, the car slewed round, left the road, and headed for a huge boab tree. Instinctively she grabbed at the wheel and realised with a shock that Don had been falling asleep.

The car came to a jerky stop, and not a moment too soon. Don was furious with himself. Glancing at him, Ashleigh saw that his face was flushed and his eyes were bloodshot.

"Oh Don! We should have stayed in Broome if you weren't feeling well," she exclaimed and blinked unbelievingly when he told her to shut up, that recriminations were useless. Recriminations? Had what she'd said sounded more than mildly reproachful? She hadn't meant it to, but probably it was the way he was feeling that was making him touchy, so she didn't protest. All the same, she didn't like the thought of him driving on if he was likely to fall asleep, and she changed her tactics.

"Sorry. I suppose it's been hard work concentrating. Where are we now, Don?"

He produced a map and showed her their exact position, as if to prove that he knew what he was doing and that he had his wits about him. But his finger shook and she could see that his hands were sweaty. Her heart sank.

"You needn't worry. I know the way to Wyuna Downs practically blindfolded."

They got back onto the road again, and for the next little while Ashleigh sat tensely, watching the track and occasionally flicking a quick look at Don to make sure he wasn't dropping off again.

When once again his steering became erratic, she knew she'd have to do something about it or they'd finish up in real trouble.

"Do let me drive, Don. I've watched what you do and I know where all the controls are. I do have my license, you know," she added half humourously.

"All right," he said grudgingly. "I suppose I need a sleep and we haven't time to stop." He unfolded the map again and went over the route laboriously, stopping every few seconds to ask Ashleigh if she was following. Her eye suddenly picked up a name—Crystal Downs—and her heart gave a lurch. So that was where Ryan Langton's cattle run was! On the map it looked to be not that far from Wyuna Downs, but she knew very well that the distances were deceptive and that the two properties were probably a long way apart.

"Pass by that track, and take the next one—don't worry if it looks as if it leads nowhere," Don was saying so emphatically she knew it must be important, and her eyes returned hastily to his pointing finger. "Just keep on and you'll see a huge boab—a double one, like twins. That's where you turn off again, a couple of kilometres on down the track. It's not much of a road but there's a sign: *Wyuna Downs*. Have you got all that? Don't miss that first track, for Pete's sake, or God knows where we'll finish up. Just keep your eyes skinned."

Ashleigh nodded and promised she would, but Don looked at her doubtfully.

"I reckon you'd better wake me in half an hour. I'll be okay by then."

"All right," Ashleigh agreed, and a couple of minutes later she was behind the wheel while Don lolled back against the seat beside her. In no time at all, he was asleep.

As she grew accustomed to the steering and to the weight of the vehicle, she began to enjoy herself. This was what she wanted: to test herself, to do something adventurous. This was why she'd left Perth, in fact. To unearth the real Ashleigh Stevens, the daughter of a girl who'd left home at nineteen—as Ashleigh was now—to drive round Australia in a combi van. Only Jackie, her mother, had got no further than Kalgoorlie in the southwest, because there she'd met Tom Stevens, who was prospecting for gold, and married him. Despite the disapproval of her wealthy parents, they'd had ten happy years. Then, when Ashleigh was nine, they'd died together in a small-plane crash. Esme had taken charge of Ashleigh after that, and had kept her so safe it was like being in a cage. But now Ashleigh was out of the cage and she intended to stay out of it.

She cast a look at Don. He was so heavily asleep she knew it would be madness to wake him and ask him to take over the driving again. Anyhow, she could cope— even though she'd never driven a heavy car like this before. At least there was no traffic to bother her!

The country was very rugged and rocky now, and there were innumerable creeks to be crossed. Sometimes they were completely dry, nothing more than

wide sandy beds with a few paper-barks growing down
the middle. Sometimes there were shallow pools to be
splashed through cautiously. The road was rose red,
fringed by long pink grasses, and the white trunks of
gums made fantastic splashes against the craggy slopes
of the savage, dark-coloured rocks. There were paper-
barks and bloodwoods too, and boabs of all different
shapes and sizes. Scattered amongst them were huge
termite mounds, their varied colours matching the
colour of the earth.

Once she saw a dingo standing beside the track,
staring at her; later there were wild donkeys. But it was
the birds that fascinated her the most: flocks of black
cockatoos, saucy rose-breasted galahs, a pair of long-
legged brolgas, wings half-spread as they bounced
along in a kind of dance through the long grass.

She drove slowly, because of the roughness of the
road, and because of the bulldust that Don had sworn
at once or twice. "Get into that," he'd said, "and you
can knock the steering to Jericho, or worse."

Poor Don! She hoped he wasn't going to be really ill.
Except that it would be fun to stay at Wyuna Downs for
a couple of days. Against her will, her thoughts veered
to Ryan Langton, though it was unlikely that she'd ever
meet up with him again. People on cattle stations must
visit each other sometimes, but he was in Broome still,
as far as she knew. She had a hauntingly clear mental
picture of his face, and suddenly the memory of what it
had been like in his arms the night before began to
surge back disturbingly into her mind. What had he
done after he'd left her? Gone to Debra, she thought
cynically, while she'd lain alone in her bed, feeling all
churned up and frustrated.

When Don was over this bout of flu or whatever it
was he had, things would be different, she told herself
with an optimism that somehow didn't go really deep.

With a sigh, she began to concentrate on her sur-

roundings again. Had she passed that track Don had
warned her to ignore? Was she, in fact, closer to the
turn-off to Wyuna Downs than she suspected? Because
there was a huge boab ahead—grotesque and bulbous,
its great trunk knotted and scarred. A double one, Don
had said, like twins. Or were there two separate boabs
there? Suddenly she was full of uncertainty.

She began to watch for the sign to Wyuna Downs, to
keep her eyes skinned. But no sign of any kind appeared, and it was just on sundown. The sky was
flowing with red colour, and soon it would be dark.
She'd forgotten they were so close to the Central
Australian time zone—an hour and a half ahead of
western standard time, and she was suddenly and
acutely aware that she was in some of the wildest and
emptiest cattle country in Australia. She wondered
uneasily if she'd missed some vital point in the information Don had given her; but it was no use panicking,
and that sign might be just ahead.

She heard cockatoos screeching and knew she must
be near water, though Don hadn't mentioned that. She
rounded a curve and there it was, in a wide creek bed,
lying in pools that looked as red as blood and streaked
with silver lead. She took the car gently down the slope.
Pandanus palms and paper-barks swarmed closely
along the bank and three pelicans drummed along the
water, then lifted themselves clumsily into the air. A
brolga picked about daintily until, disturbed by the car,
it too took to the air, trailing its long legs neatly and
elegantly behind.

It was because she was watching the birds that she
didn't notice the rocks in the dazzlingly red water that
scattered into streaks and fragments as the car plunged
in.

A moment later there was a terrible thump. Don
lurched against her and groaned, but didn't wake, and
her heart pounded. What had that thump meant? She'd

hit something big—and hit it hard. Oh God—she hoped she hadn't done any damage to the car. At least it was still going on through the water, and as it splashed through the last stretch and she steered it up through the trees on the sloping bank at the other side, she gave a sigh of relief—too soon. The car heaved itself along a little way and stopped dead. Panic! Ashleigh pushed Don's bulk away from her and climbed out to rush round and open the bonnet. She knew nothing about car engines; she'd always depended on garages and mechanics. Now there was no garage, no mechanic. No cattle station either. And Don would be ropeable when he came to and found what she'd done. Her opinion of herself as a girl who could cope with adventure was going rapidly down the drain.

She felt tears flood her eyes and dashed them away furiously. This was one time when tears weren't going to get her anywhere.

"Don!" She leaned in the window of the car and shook him hard and his eyes rolled open and he stared at her as if he didn't even know who she was. He looked really sick.

There was still some tea left in the thermos. With shaking hands, she poured some into a mug and offered it to him with some aspirin she had in her hold-all. To her relief, he seemed to be quite conscious now. He drank some of the tea; then it seemed to strike him that something was wrong.

"What are we stopping here for? Where the hell are we? It's nearly dark! We should have reached Wyuna Downs by now."

"I know, Don," Ashleigh said, almost in tears. "But something's gone wrong with the car. It won't go. I—I hit something in the creek bed—"

She stopped at the expression on his face.

"The sump. You must have busted a hole in it."

She stared at him blankly. She had only a vague idea of what the sump was, but busting it sounded pretty serious from the way Don spoke.

"I'll go for help," she said, rummaging for the map and the torch. "If you'll just show me where we are—"

He pushed the map aside. "I don't know where the hell we are. It's as black as pitch and for all I know you've been driving back towards Derby."

"I haven't," she said. At least she knew that. She knew that the sun had set behind them; there were remnants of a savage gory sunset still in the sky, and it wasn't black as pitch at all. "We shouldn't have left Broome if you weren't feeling well anyhow," she accused, and Don glared at her.

"Don't try to put the blame on me, Leigh. I was okay when we left. You should have wakened me if you'd lost your bearings." He got out of the car and staggered slightly. "We're stuck here for the night, that's for sure. Give me the torch."

She handed it to him and watched him as he looked briefly under the bonnet, his forehead glistening with sweat in the eerie torch-light. Then he crawled under the vehicle.

"It's the bloody sump all right," he said as he emerged.

"What can we do?" she asked huskily.

"Nothing. Not a damned thing. . . . What the hell were you thinking of? You must have driven straight on top of a great gooly."

Ashleigh moistened her lips. Yes, she'd done exactly that and it was too late for regrets.

"There are sleeping bags in the boot. While you're getting them, get the water-bag too. I'm as dry as a crow," Don snapped.

Silently, she did as he asked her, then went back for what was left of their picnic lunch. But Don didn't want anything to eat. All he was interested in was water. Then, without any explanation, he staggered off into the darkness—to relieve himself, she supposed.

He came back a few minutes later to grab up one of the sleeping bags, zip it open, and crawl into it on the ground near the car. He was shivering, Ashleigh noticed as she held the torch for him helpfully, yet the night was warm. In seconds she could tell by his heavy breathing that he was asleep. Ashleigh tidied away the remains of the picnic box, then decided there was nothing for it but to follow his example—except that she wasn't asleep in seconds. The ground was hard, and the thought of curling up in the car was tempting, but out here she could keep an eye on Don. She stared up at the sky, worrying about the predicament they were in, but soon her thoughts drifted compulsively to Ryan Langton and last night. Somehow it seemed impossible that she'd never see him again. . . .

She was startled out of her thoughts by the sound of Don's groans. She crawled out of her sleeping bag and leaned over him anxiously.

"Don—what is it?" She could see his dark, bearded face in the starlight, his eyes like black holes, open but not seeing her.

"Water," he croaked, like some dying man in the desert, and she hurried for the water-bag. He drank, then went back to sleep again.

Ashleigh thought the night would never end. Oh, it was beautiful here, the shadows and shapes were fantastic and she was not in the least frightened, but it was impossible to keep from worrying about Don. Ashleigh tried to plan what she'd do in the morning: scout around to see if there were any signs of civilisation, light a fire of green stuff to create a smoke signal. . . .

She opened her eyes, roused by a small sound. She must have slept and now—incredibly—the night was over. Don had emerged from his sleeping bag and was getting clumsily to his feet.

She sat up at once. "Don—are you feeling better?"

He didn't answer, but walked off towards the trees the way he'd done last night.

Ashleigh scrambled out of her sleeping bag. She hadn't dared to undress, and her clothes—her pale blue pants and blue-and-mauve striped blouse—were unspeakably crumpled. But who cared? There was certainly no one to see. They were in a small valley, hemmed in by steep red cliffs, the white trunks of snappy gums and the grotesque shapes of boabs standing out against them. Wild passionfruit vines draped the trees, their small orange-coloured fruit making bright splashes of colour, and as a flock of black cockatoos with red tails flew across the pale blue of the sky, she caught her breath. It was like a primitive Eden, where Adam and Eve would have had shining black bodies, she thought, and for a fleeting moment she was completely entranced.

Then, as her gaze wandered through the trees, she saw Don. He was clambering awkwardly across the rocks at the foot of the cliffs, and her blood froze. What on earth was he doing? Was he delirious?

She began running quickly towards him.

"Don!" she called in alarm.

He turned sharply, then staggered, flung out his arms and fell, his body thudding to the ground at the foot of the huge rock he'd been standing on.

Ashleigh ran towards him, panting and frightened because he hadn't gotten up.

"Oh Don!" She dropped to her knees beside him. "Are you all right?" She wiped the sweat from his forehead as she spoke, using the handkerchief that protruded from his shirt pocket. The black cockatoos screamed raucously from the trees where they'd settled, and she didn't hear what Don muttered as he sat

up. He tried to get to his feet, then sank back helplessly.

"My leg—I can't move it. . . . For God's sake leave
it alone, leave it alone," he snapped out, though
Ashleigh had made the merest movement towards him.

"Is it broken?" she asked, agonised.

Through his teeth he replied, "I haven't a clue. All I
know is I can't move it."

"Oh Don—what can I do?" she breathed.

"Nothing . . . unless you feel like climbing up to the
top of that cliff," he said curtly. "You might be able to
see if there's a windmill, a dam, cattle. Horses, people,
anything. That's what I was about to do when you
yelled out as though you'd been bitten by a snake or
something."

Ashleigh could have wept. Couldn't she do anything
right? She turned away and scrambled over the rocks.
She could see there was a rough track going up the cliff,
and she began to climb up it, slowly and cautiously. If
she fell and broke her leg too, they would really be in
the soup.

Panting and perspiring, she finally reached the top of
the cliff and stood there looking around her. As far as
she could see—and she could see a long long way—
there was nothing. Only acres and acres of waving
Mitchell grass stretching out to the horizon. Plus a few
termite mounds. Or were they cattle? One of the dark
shapes moved and she knew it must be a cow or a bull
or a steer, or something. At any rate, they were on
somebody's cattle run.

She made her way back to Don, taking her time,
going backwards down the steepest parts of the path.

"There are some cattle over there, Don. . . . What
shall I do? Will you be all right if I leave you on your
own and try to get help?"

He was shivering again, huddled on the ground and
looking terrible. "Get my sleeping bag—I'm cold."

She couldn't get any further sense out of him, and for the next little while she was completely occupied trying to make him comfortable. When at last he fell asleep, she'd reached the conclusion that the best thing to do would be to make a fire and try to send an SOS that way. She hadn't seen any men riding around with the cattle, but there was at least a chance that smoke would be seen by somebody, somewhere.

As soon as she'd collected a reasonably big pile of leaves and green branches, she lit the fire, using newspaper from the car to start it. She watched it begin to smoulder, and then smoke trailed up into the blue sky and gradually blossomed into a cloud.

Eagerly she began gathering more green fuel, ready to pile it on as soon as the smoke cloud grew less. She was dirty and perspiring, and she'd torn her blouse and her face felt grimy in the heat of the sun. She'd put on her pretty straight-brimmed straw hat because she didn't want to be burned to a cinder, but it wasn't standing up to the strain too well. She knocked it sideways jumping up when she heard the sound of a motor—just when she'd used the last of her fuel and was wondering if she could possibly summon the strength to collect any more.

Dazed and disbelieving, uncertain whether she was hallucinating or not, she began to run along the barely discernible wheel track that meandered through the valley.

A dust-covered Land Rover came into sight through the trees and she stood in the middle of the track and waved her arms like a maniac.

The Land Rover pulled up abruptly a yard away from her, the car door opened, and she nearly died of shock when Ryan Langton appeared.

# Chapter Three

Ashleigh stared at him as though he were an apparition. The civilised look he'd had when they met in Broome had disappeared and her heart pounded as she met his eyes. He wore a light khaki shirt, narrow-legged pants, and tan boots, and his thick black hair was ruffled and untidy. He came striding towards her, his hands on his narrow hips, those startling aquamarine eyes taking her in from her rakish straw hat to her pretty pants, both of them streaked with smoke from the fire.

"Ashleigh Stevens." He said it slowly. "What the hell are you doing here on my property—looking as though you've spent the last few hours fighting bush-fires?"

Ashleigh wanted to laugh hysterically at the expression on his face, but oh! it was heaven that help had come, and that it should be someone she—she knew.

"You saw the smoke," she said, her voice trembling. "I didn't know if anyone would—or if it was wrong to light a fire here, and I couldn't ask Don because—" She knew she was gabbling and she stopped as he took hold of her arm and shook her roughly.

"What's this all about? Come on now, pull yourself together—"

"Don—Don's hurt," she stammered.

"Hurt? Don't you mean he's sick? Where is he?"

"He fell—he hurt his leg—he can't walk. He's over there near the rocks." She had him by the arm now, but she was beyond electrical reactions. She was suddenly overwhelmingly thankful that she and Don weren't going to die of heat and thirst and hunger in the outback, a melodramatic fear that had been lurking deep down in her mind all this time and had only now floated up to the surface.

Don had his eyes open when she and Ryan reached him and he too stared unbelievingly.

"Don't tell me we're on your cattle run!"

He looked accusingly at Ashleigh, and Ryan asked abruptly, "What's the trouble?"

Ashleigh could tell what he was thinking by the coldness of his voice: Don shouldn't have left Broome when he was sick.

Don scowled. "I've done something to my leg—twisted it. Ashleigh crashed the car into a boulder and we've been stranded here all night. I was going to climb up the cliff to look around this morning and—"

"And I called out and he—he turned round and lost his footing," Ashleigh said quickly, before Don could say it.

"Let's have a look."

Ryan crouched down as he spoke, and Don said, "Looking's no use to me. I need a doctor—a hospital."

Ryan took no notice. He was feeling Don's knee and after a minute he pronounced, "You've cracked your knee-cap." He stood up. "I'm going to make a splint of sorts and then we'll get you into the back of the Land

Rover and take you to the homestead. I'll contact my sister and ask her to get the air ambulance out from Kununurra."

He turned away and Ashleigh tried to smile at Don and found that tears of relief were running down her face.

"For Pete's sake, don't cry," he said irritably. "How do you think that's going to help?" Don grumbled.

It wasn't. She spent the next three minutes sniffing back her tears and composing herself. It was disturbing to find she was so weak. So *soft.* Just as Debra Davis had said—one little adventure and she was in pieces.

Ryan came back in the Land Rover, manoeuvring it into a position as near to Don as possible. He produced a straight piece of wood plus some rag from the back of the car and immobilised Don's leg with the improvised splint. Then with a little help from Ashleigh, though she was aware he could have managed perfectly well on his own, he got Don into the back of the vehicle.

"What about our . . . Don's car?" she asked, hesitantly. "Are you going to tow it back with you?"

"No, I'm not. Your friend's going to have a rough enough ride as it is. . . . Show me what you want from the car: Don's stuff, yours as well. You'd better go with him in the ambulance."

Yes of course she had. Poor Don! Her blood froze when she thought of the mess she'd landed them in. And somehow to have Ryan Langton witness it made it worse than ever, though it would have been even more terrible if it had been Debra, she admitted to herself.

The luggage was stowed away; then Ashleigh climbed into the front passenger seat and sank back—exhausted, tearful, finished. Ryan got in beside her and they drove off slowly.

"How did you manage to find your way here?" he asked her presently, his voice so low that Don couldn't have heard even if he were listening—which, by the look of him, he was not. She gritted her teeth, aware that he was implying she'd come here deliberately. But for heaven's sake, it had been the purest accident!

She turned her head to say something biting and encountered the blueness of his gaze for the merest fraction of a second, which was still long enough for something drastic to happen to her physical being, exhausted though she was, and for her to blush a fiery red.

She looked away from him hastily. "I didn't *manage* to find my way here, whatever that means. I missed the turn off, that's all. We were going to Wyuna Downs. Don has friends there."

Ryan laughed softly. "Then you're so far off course it isn't funny. . . . You were driving, weren't you?"

Yes she'd been driving, and no it wasn't funny. And she wasn't going to discuss it. She moved slightly and her thigh touched his. He shifted his leg immediately and she froze. He thought she'd meant to do that. And she hadn't.

He glanced at her sideways, and she knew her colour was high. "You look like you've got a fever, Ashleigh. You'll probably be hospitalised too. That will be convenient, won't it?"

Would it? Who for? Her or him?

"I don't know what you mean," she murmured indistinctly, and he didn't bother to elucidate.

They travelled slowly along the track for some distance and had emerged into open country again when Ryan said interestedly, "Didn't you have a map that you fetched up on my cattle run? I must admit you have me really puzzled."

Ashleigh squirmed and bit her lip. "You don't have to be puzzled," she said tiredly. "You needn't flatter yourself I did it on purpose. As I'm sure Debra would tell you, I'm just not capable of coping with the outback—even with the aid of a map, which I find it just a little difficult to study while I'm driving," she finished with a flourish.

"Of course you wouldn't think of pulling up," he commented. "In my frank opinion, you shouldn't have been driving."

Oh no, Ashleigh thought. Not another man who disliked women drivers!

"Not that I have anything against women drivers," he went on, as if he knew exactly what she was thinking, "but out here driving is hard work, and you look as fragile as if you'd blow away when the breeze comes up at sundown."

"If you think that, you're wrong," Ashleigh said argumentatively. "If I wanted to be here—which I don't—it would take a cyclone to blow me away, Mr. Langton."

"Then you'd better not want to be here," he countered, his mouth twisting. "The fact is, you don't know a damned thing about the bush."

"I'm learning," she said under her breath, thinking of last night, thinking· how she'd felt this morning, stranded there in the middle of emptiness with a man who'd put his leg out of action. She could have had hysterics—but she hadn't. Though she didn't suppose she was going to get any credit for that.

"You people who don't know what you're about and break down on cattle stations have no idea what a nuisance you make of yourselves," Ryan continued.

Ashleigh broke in angrily, "Then I'm sorry. Maybe you'd better let me out here—and Don too. I suppose he shouldn't have needed a sleep, and I shouldn't have given him a break and taken a turn driving. So go ahead—tip us out—"

"Oh quit the histrionics," he said wearily. "You know I'm not going to tip you out, so calm down. As for your friend snoring in the back there, he's just as much to blame as you. He ought to have considered your lack of experience before he left Broome, in his state of health."

"I suppose you never make mistakes," Ashleigh snapped. She was blinking back tears and determined he wouldn't see them. She felt at a hideous disadvantage, looking as she did and with her battered hat still perched on her head. She snatched it off angrily. She'd paid a lot for that hat and now it was ruined. "I expect you wouldn't let any woman—not even Debra Davis— drive any car you were travelling in." She heard the tears in her voice and hated *him* for hearing them too.

"Debra's to be trusted," he said shortly.

Ashleigh thought, Oh yes—Debra could be trusted. She came from a frontier city, she could do everything. She slumped back in the seat and closed her eyes.

"You're sickening with the same virus that's attacked your friends," Ryan said after what seemed an age, during which time Ashleigh's thoughts had gone round and round in a kind of whirlpool, from sheer exhaustion. "With a little luck the air ambulance will drop down on my air-strip in half an hour or so and you and Don can be on your way."

"Leigh's not coming with me." Don spoke groggily but positively from the back of the Land Rover. "Someone has to get the car out of here when it's been repaired, and it's certainly not going to be me."

Ashleigh glanced at Ryan. There was sense in what Don said. She would have to wait around. But Ryan said nothing. It was as if Don hadn't even spoken. His face was set—hard, implacable; quite obviously he wasn't going to invite her to stay.

Nobody spoke for several minutes after that. Then Ryan remarked flatly, "We're going to call into the homestead. My sister might enjoy your company while you're waiting for the air ambulance."

"Might she?" said Ashleigh remotely. That would be a change! If it was true, she thought. It didn't seem

Ryan was exactly enjoying their company, and frankly, she wasn't particularly interested in entertaining his sister, if she were anything like Ryan. All she wanted was to go straight out to the air-strip. Ryan could dump them there. They'd wait for the ambulance to come and he could disappear in the nearest puff of smoke. As for the car, she and Don would work out something about that between them.

"You'll find it more pleasant waiting in the garden at all events," Ryan said as if he hadn't the slightest idea of the way she was feeling. "There's no shade on the air-strip."

"I see. That's thoughtful of you." She nearly choked on the insincerity. She was bitterly, bitterly hurt, for some reason or other. There she'd been this morning, buzzing around, doing her best for Don, messing up her clothes and her hands and her nails, and worried sick about everything. Now she suddenly was being treated as a nuisance, a menace, and being packed off without even the tiniest pat on the back for—well, for sending up that smoke signal. But of course she had no right to feel hurt by Ryan's attitude to her, his impatience to be rid of her. She meant nothing to him. As for that magnetic attraction or whatever it was that had drawn them together briefly, quite positively it wasn't working any more. They must be in the wrong magnetic field, she decided wryly.

She wondered suddenly if Debra Davis were at Crystal Downs, taking time off to celebrate the completion of her assignment or something, and possibly her engagement to Ryan Langton as well.

When at last the homestead came into view, it was a surprise. Ashleigh had expected something quite different, but as they drove through the big tropical garden crowded with palms and peppercorns and exotic shade trees, to say nothing of brightly flowered shrubs, she discovered it was an elegant two-storied building. The roof was a soft grey-green, the walls were painted cream; upstairs was balconied, downstairs there was a verandah wreathed in vines. It looked cool, welcoming.

That was, of course, if you could forget the boss, who was certainly cool, but not in the least welcoming. His sister sounded more friendly, and Ashleigh hoped she was. She could do with a little friendliness just now.

Ryan drove the car halfway round the gravel drive, pulling up in the shade of huge Indian rain trees. They were called that, Ashleigh knew, because of the way the long dry pods rattled at certain times of the year, making a sound like rain on the roof. On the lawn under the same trees was a table covered with a white-and-yellow checked cloth, where cups and saucers were set out around a big plate of scones.

Ryan got out of the car and Ashleigh followed, not waiting for him to open her door for her. She felt very conscious of her bedraggled appearance and wondered what his sister would be like—if she were older than Ryan and as forceful. She glanced in at Don, lying in the back of the Land Rover, his roughly splinted leg stretched out stiffly, his bearded face flushed and sweaty. She'd never seen him at such a disadvantage before; it was a little pathetic, somehow. She went close to him and asked him quietly, gently, "Are you okay, Don?"

He opened his eyes and nodded. "I'll be glad to see the doc," he mumbled.

"It shouldn't be long now," she said reassuringly. When she turned away, someone came out of the house: a young woman who looked to be in her late twenties, with straight fair hair and lightly tanned skin. She was tallish and slim, and she wore a blue denim skirt and a white cotton blouse.

"My sister, Gene Fleming," Ryan said. "Gene, this is Ashleigh Stevens. And the patient, Don Harris."

"Hello!" Gene's smile was definitely friendly. "You

look as though you've been having a rough time. I guess you'd like a wash and a change of clothing while I'm making the tea, Ashleigh."

"If it's possible," Ashleigh said, smiling back and hoping Ryan wouldn't say she didn't have time for that. She didn't fancy the idea of landing at the hospital looking the way she did at present, especially when there were clean clothes in her suitcase.

"I'll be with you in a moment," Gene said, and leaned in at the car window. "How's the patient? Ryan says you've broken your knee-cap. How about I give you some pain-killer while you're waiting for the ambulance?"

"Don't bother. My leg's not painful, it's just useless. A cup of tea's all I want; I'll leave any other treatment to the doctor." Don hadn't managed a smile and Ashleigh didn't altogether blame him, though she thought he might have tried to sound a little more appreciative of Gene's offer.

"One cup of tea coming up," Gene said breezily. "Come on inside, Ashleigh. You can use one of the bedrooms upstairs. Ryan will bring your suitcase or whatever you want. . . . Where were you heading for when this happened?" she continued, as Ashleigh followed her up the steps and across a verandah with a cool stone floor.

"We're on our way to Darwin, actually. But we were going to spend the night at Wyuna Downs, with friends of Don's."

Gene's eyebrows disappeared under her blonde fringe. "You did get off the track! I take it you're new to the Kimberleys. You practically need to be born here to find your way around." She led Ashleigh across a hallway with a polished hardwood floor in the direction of a carpeted stairway. Behind them the screen door on the verandah banged shut as Ryan came in, presumably with her suitcase, Ashleigh thought, but she didn't turn to check.

"What are you going to do in Darwin? Have a holiday?"

"No. Don's buying out Jabiru Safari Tours, and I'm going to hostess for him."

"Really?" Gene looked surprised. "Are you sure you'll like it?"

"Pretty sure," Ashleigh said evenly, aware that Ryan was just behind them.

They reached the top of the stairs and another wide, rectangular hallway, off which several doors opened.

"Why don't you stay here with us for a few nights, until you know what's happening?" Gene asked, pausing in the middle of the hall. "It's not much fun to be all alone in a part of the country you don't know." She turned to her brother. "Wouldn't that be a good idea, Ryan?"

Ashleigh went crimson. She knew already that Ryan didn't think it would be a good idea. Before he could speak, she said hastily, "Thank you. But I'd rather go in the plane with Don."

"Oh, but why?" Gene asked, and Ryan said curtly, "Because, my dear Gene, Ashleigh is shortly going to qualify for hospitalisation too."

Ashleigh bit back a denial. She was not about to qualify for hospitalisation. There was nothing at all wrong with her. Whatever virus it was that had attacked Laura and Don was not attacking her. But what was the use of telling Ryan Langton that? He was sure to know better. He was also sure to suspect that she was angling for an invitation, which she was not. She'd much prefer to go with Don. Which reminded her . . . so far, there'd been no sign of Debra Davis. . . .

Gene pushed open a door, frowning slightly. "In

here, Ashleigh. The bathroom's right opposite, and there are clean towels on the rail. You're not sick, are you?"

Ashleigh shook her head. She'd caught a glimpse of herself in the mirror over the dressing table. She was not a pretty sight. Her clothes were not only crumpled from being slept in, they were also definitely the worse from her dealings with the fire. Even apart from that, her eyes looked too big and too black, and her face was smeared with dirt. To cap it all, she suddenly discovered she was clutching the battered straw hat that had once been so elegant and pretty, and she hid it quickly behind her back—not because Gene was staring at her, but because Ryan was.

"So what's it all about? I'm afraid I don't get it," Gene remarked. She looked challengingly at Ryan, and he said tersely, "You don't have any powers of observation, do you, Gene?"

He dumped the suitcase on the end of the bed and in the brief interval before he turned round again, Gene's dark-blue eyes, which were not in the least like Ryan's, ran rapidly down Ashleigh's figure and came to a full stop on her flat stomach. Ashleigh swallowed down an angry laugh. For heaven's sake! Did she think Ryan meant she was pregnant?

"I'm not—" she began, and Ryan said at exactly the same moment, "Didn't you notice that Ashleigh's friend has a nasty virus as well as a split knee-cap?"

*Ashleigh's friend.* Some intonation in his voice as he said that made it sound as if she and Don were a lot more than mere friends. Her nostrils dilated slightly.

Gene wrinkled her forehead. "Now I come to think of it, he did look a bit flushed. I thought it was just the heat." She sent Ashleigh a look that was apologetic, but also speculative, and Ashleigh could guess why that was. "Well, I'll go down and see about the tea."

She vanished, and Ryan said coldly, "Don't take too

long over your *toilette*, Ashleigh. I daresay you want to reconstitute your image, but I'll expect you to be ready to leave the minute we hear the plane."

"I'll be ready," Ashleigh said equally coldly. "Don't get the idea I want to linger on in the—the warmth of your hospitality."

"I'll try not to do that," he agreed. His eyes flicked down to her hand then back to her face. "And by the way . . . that hat of yours. There's a lesson to be learned there."

"What?" she demanded, her fingers tightening on the broken smoke-blackened brim.

"That the north's a very different place from Perth," he said.

Ashleigh gritted her teeth. "I picked that up long ago. Also the fact that the men up here are very different," she added incoherently.

"Very different," he agreed.

They stared at each other and in just three seconds she had to look away. Infuriatingly, incomprehensibly, her bones were beginning to melt around the edges.

With a brief movement, she turned her back and snapped open her suitcase. She rummaged in it until she heard him leave the room, and then she collapsed on the bed.

Her mind, her emotions were in a turmoil. She wished it had been someone else who'd materialised in answer to her smoke signal. Someone helpful and innocuous, instead of a man who knocked her sideways every time he looked at her and whom she *liked* less every time she saw him.

But at least it was teaching her something: that physical attraction was a snare and a delusion. She'd sooner a man like Don any day, even if thoughts of going to bed with him didn't pop in and out of her head. No one could say Don wasn't human. He'd been a little unfair in the way he blamed her for the accident, but

there was some excuse for him. He was sick. And as
well, there was the matter of his pride, she thought
shrewdly. It must be embarrassing for someone like
him to have such an accident happen to him. Anyhow,
it didn't make her like him any less. Ryan Langton—in
spite of his self-assurance, his desperately fascinating
blue eyes—had no heart, no real feelings. Debra Davis
was welcome to every little bit of him. . . .

She crossed to the window and looked outside.
Beyond the garden a vast tree-scattered tract of country
stretched away out to the horizon, where low ragged
ranges broke the sky line. How big was this cattle run?
she wondered. Half a million acres? In spite of everything, she couldn't help getting a certain thrill out of
being here, even if it was only for an hour or so. She
didn't feel in the least like a fly that had fallen into a jug
of milk, she thought with a faint smile.

She turned away from the window and decided to
take a shower. She'd be quick—not because of Ryan's
injunctions, but for Don's sake. He wouldn't want to be
waiting around in the Land Rover once the plane came
in.

It was hunger as well as consideration for Don that
got her through her shower in double-quick time. She
wanted a cup of tea, and she wanted some of those
scones. In the bedroom, she hunted out a vanilla skirt
and a plain blue top with a deep cardigan neckline.
Pretty and fragile, her kind of clothes, she thought, and
was aware of mixed feelings about that.

She was in her half slip and bra, combing her damp
hair at the mirror when Ryan pushed open the door and
stood looking at her across the room.

She blushed hotly and swung around.

"You didn't knock! What do you want?"

His eyes ran over her deliberately and she felt her
breast move as she took a deep breath. She was
perfectly decent, far more so than if she'd been wearing

a bikini, but all the same, she didn't like being looked at that way. Or . . . or did she? Exactly what did that stirring at the pit of her stomach mean? It certainly had nothing to do with being hungry, at any rate.

"I came to see if your luggage is ready," he said, and she thought instantly, Liar. That wasn't what had brought him here. It was something else, but he wasn't going to admit to it. It was me, she thought. The thought was so vivid she couldn't look at him. She didn't know why it had come into her head, unless he'd put it there, the way he was looking at her.

"No, it's not ready," she said shakily. "Just let me finish dressing, will you? The plane hasn't come, has it?"

"No." His aquamarine eyes were startlingly jewel-like against the tan of his face, and she glanced away from him quickly. "You're looking very exquisite again, now you've showered."

Ashleigh moistened her lips. Why did he have to say something like that? Why didn't he just go away, instead of staying here and stirring her up?

But he didn't go away. He moved across the room and stopped mere inches from her, while she stood with her back pressed to the edge of the dressing table, her nostrils slightly dilated, her black lashes veiling the darkness of her eyes. Every sensible thought had gone out of her head, every thought about disliking him, about wishing she'd never set eyes on him again, about getting out of here. She heard herself swallow and she raised her eyes and looked fully into his.

This time, she didn't look away. She couldn't. Not until his arms were around her and his mouth was on hers, hungrily, possessively. She closed her eyes and let it all happen. Let herself cling to him, delight in the pressure of his body against her own. Let herself savour to the full the strength of her desire for him—and his for her.

She seemed hardly to be breathing when he released her, but her eyes were on his again and there was a big question in her mind demanding to be asked—the sort of question she'd never entertained before but that was in complete possession of her mind, of her whole being, now.

"What are we going to do?"

Had she actually whispered the words? She must have, because he answered her, his voice clipped, although his eyes were still dark with passion.

"Not another thing, Ashleigh. That's as far as it goes—and that's too far."

"But—but why? What do you mean?" she choked, wanting nothing except to be back in his arms again.

"I mean that I have a few moral standards, even if you haven't," he said tersely. "Not that I'm putting all the blame on you, God knows. . . . Let's just—forget it, that's all."

Ashleigh felt sickened. He'd dropped her just like this in Broome. And how he could she didn't know—not when they'd both been feeling the way they had. Yet exactly what had he been feeling? What did she know about men? Nothing, she thought helplessly. Don hadn't taught her a thing. And—she'd forgotten all about Don. It was frightening. . . .

She stood staring up at him, her eyes dazed, her heart thumping, while he confirmed her naivety.

"If you had any sense, Miss Ashleigh Stevens, you'd cut your losses and run. Now. Instead of looking at me that way. I'll get your bag later, when you come down. And for God's sake, when you're leaving, don't kiss me good bye."

He went. And Ashleigh hated him for what he'd said, and for knowing what she felt; hated herself for feeling it. She was a slow learner, she guessed. As for moral standards, she hadn't asked him to break in on her while she was dressing. He was a dangerous man, and she was thankful she'd be leaving shortly.

She dragged on her top and skirt and slammed her suitcase shut. The fact was, she didn't know how to play such grown-up games. She didn't know the rules. Or the penalties.

Nor did she know a thing about the man she was playing with—or was it against? Except that it seemed to turn her into a different person just to look at him, and not a person she particularly admired. Definitely not.

# Chapter Four

Funnily enough, when she went downstairs, Ashleigh was still hungry. But that could be because Ryan Langton wasn't around. She had her tea and her scones—four of them, lusciously fresh and oozing with butter.

"Did you make these?" she asked Gene. "They're brilliant!"

"Don't give me the credit. I got Selma to run them up when I heard from Ryan. She's the mechanic's wife. I gave Don some aspirin, by the way. He's dozing now, so that's a good thing. . . . Now tell me how you came to be stranded at Little Valley. Ryan's as closed as an oyster. He hasn't told me a thing. Was Don driving?"

Ashleigh grimaced. "No, I was. It was all my fault. Don was asleep—he wasn't feeling well—and I must have missed the turn off to Wyuna Downs. And then I collided with a rock when I was crossing a creek and made a hole in the sump." She bit her lip. Put like that,

Ashleigh could see she hadn't come out of her first encounter with the outback very well. It was no wonder Ryan had made that crack about people who didn't understand the bush making a nuisance of themselves.

"And what about Don's knee?" Gene prompted. "How did that happen?"

"Oh, that wasn't 'til this morning. We had to sleep out last night you see and I suppose that didn't help Don's fever. Then at first light, he tried to climb up the cliff to see where we were. I shouldn't have let him, of course, and I was stupid enough to call out and he slipped and smashed his knee-cap."

"Don't blame yourself for everything," Gene exclaimed. "It was hardly your fault Don slipped. And you did have the good sense to light a fire. Or was that Don's idea?" she added, rather cynically.

Ashleigh flushed at her tone. "No, it was my idea. . . . I nearly fell over when it was Ryan who came to the rescue. I hadn't the slightest idea we were on Crystal Downs."

Gene stared at her. "Do you mean you and Ryan have actually met before? And he never said a word! Honestly, men are quite inexplicable."

Ashleigh certainly agreed with that, particularly when it came to Ryan Langton. But she wasn't going into that subject with his sister, and she said carelessly, "He probably didn't think it was worth mentioning. We met in Broome the other day, that's all. He was with Debra," she added, to show she knew just how matters stood. "Don and Debra had met before in Darwin, you see."

Before either of them could say anything further, Don called out to her from the back of the station wagon, and with a murmured excuse she hurried to see what he wanted.

"What is it, Don? Is there something I can get you?"

He shook his head. "Listen, Leigh, what have you arranged about the car?"

She widened her eyes. "I haven't arranged anything," she began, and he broke in forcibly, "You can't just walk out and forget it, you know. Particularly since the whole thing's your fault."

"No, of course not," she agreed, and wondered why she hadn't given any thought to the car. "But what can I do, Don? I can't just stay here. I haven't been invited. Ryan doesn't—"

"Oh, blow Ryan. What about that sister of his? Have you explained the situation to her? If not, then I will. And if you're going to act like your Aunt Esme and tell me it's not the thing to do to fish for an invitation, then let me remind you it's your fault there's a hole in the sump and it's also due to you I've cracked my knee. I'm not going to be able to do anything about the damned car, so you'd better dig in your heels and tell Ryan Langton that you're staying here until he gets his mechanic on the job."

Ashleigh tried to imagine herself doing that and failed. It would be much easier for Don to negotiate with him. If he could talk to her so coherently, then he could talk to Ryan. They could probably arrange to have someone else drive the car to Kununurra and she wouldn't have to stay here.

"Don, why don't you—" she began, but he interrupted her with an angry snort.

"Why don't I what? Thanks to you, I can't do a thing but lie here like a log, and—" His burning eyes left her face.

Turning her head, Ashleigh discovered that Gene had come across to the car and was standing only a few feet away. Ashleigh blushed with embarrassment as she wondered how much of their conversation had been audible, but Don was unconcerned.

"I've just been talking to Leigh about the car. I know you must have a mechanic on the property, and I know it's imposing on you to ask it, but could he get the necessary things done? Leigh doesn't seem to like to mention it. I guess she's feeling bad about her carelessness."

"Oh, don't worry," Gene assured him. "Ryan will send Charlie out to see to your car. There's no problem."

"There is if Leigh leaves on the plane with me," Don retorted. "She'll have to stay here 'til the car's on the road again. And even then she's going to need someone to help her on the way. She hasn't an ounce of road sense when it comes to driving in the outback."

Ashleigh shrank inwardly. Don was brashly taking it for granted that she could stay here, that she'd be given a bed. But she had the feeling it wasn't going to be such a pushover. It really was asking rather a lot of Ryan to expect him to have his mechanic spend time on the car and as well to find someone to escort a hopeless driver to Kununurra, though as for that, she was sure she could manage on her own.

She turned to Gene with an uneasy smile. "Ryan thinks I should go with Don in the plane," she said apologetically, and out of the corner of her eye she saw Don glaring at her angrily.

"Oh, that's only because he's concerned about your catching this virus," Gene assured her. "I think it would be a good idea for you to stay. It's only common sense, really—as Don's pointed out," she said with a dryness that gave Ashleigh the idea she wasn't much impressed with Don. Gene ran her fingers through her blonde hair and smiled sympathetically at Ashleigh. "I'll go and explain to my brother what's been decided, before he fetches your suitcase down."

And he'll tell you to think again, Ashleigh thought as

Gene walked away. Her heart was pounding, but Don looked pleased with himself.

"There you are. That's all fixed up nicely, isn't it?"

Was it? There was such a thing as counting your chickens before they were hatched, she thought cynically. Moreover, Don might not look quite so smug if he knew what had been going on upstairs a short time ago. . . .

She heard the droning of a plane, and as Gene reached the foot of the steps, Ryan appeared, her suitcase already in his hand. He flicked a quick glance in Ashleigh's direction—checking to see if she was ready to leave, she supposed. She wondered almost aloofly how he'd react to Gene's suggestion.

"Oh Ryan, you needn't have fetched that bag," she heard Gene say. "We've been talking and I've decided the best thing will be for Ashleigh to stay here until their car's been fixed. If she develops a temperature, I can look after her. It's not going to bother you, and after all, I'm the one who's all alone at the homestead while you and the boys are out at the cattle camp."

She didn't hear what Ryan said, but he dropped her bag and strode along the drive to confront Ashleigh. She quaked inwardly, but she looked straight at him as he stopped and glared at her.

"So you're staying, are you, Miss Stevens? I don't know how you imagine you're going to get that car to Kununurra. Judging by your past performance, you won't be able to find your way as far as the front gate. However, my sister's intent on having her own way. . . . Are you coming out to the air-strip?"

She stared back at him. "No thank you. I'll say good bye to Don now."

She watched him walk round to the other side of the car, and hoped she'd made the point that she didn't fancy the drive back alone with him.

Don was saying with a wry grin, "He's hard to get on with! But you'll be all right. Someone will see you get to Kununurra. And Leigh—I'm sorry I've been such a louse, but it was just one thing on top of another. You understand, don't you? No hard feelings?"

"No hard feelings," she agreed. "I hope you'll be okay, Don. I'll see you in Kununurra as soon as I can get there. And I promise you I'll be very careful. Good bye." She took his hand and pressed it, but she didn't kiss him. After all, what man can feel amorous when he has a virus plus a broken knee-cap? Certainly not Don, she told herself.

Ryan started up the car and Ashleigh discovered Gene had come to stand by her and call good bye to Don. The buzz of the plane had grown louder; shielding her eyes with her hand, Ashleigh saw that it was directly above, silvery grey against the deep blue of the sky. In no time at all Don would have gone and she'd be on her own. It wasn't what she'd planned when she'd left Perth. At the back of her mind was a niggling little doubt about the future. She'd take the hostessing job with the safari tours, of course, but she was going to have to think very carefully before she got tied up with Don. She was pretty sure that his bad temper was simply a result of the accident combined with the fact that he wasn't well, and she assured herself it would work out all right.

When the Land Rover had gone, she and Gene walked back to the house together, and she began to realise just how tired she was. She was ready to drop, in fact, in spite of the fact that she was all tensed up.

"You'd better go upstairs and get straight into bed and have a good sleep, Ashleigh," Gene said sympathetically. "You look really done in."

Ashleigh smiled wanly. She felt done in, and she wondered as she went upstairs why she'd let herself be persuaded to stay here so easily. It wasn't going to be any fun, of that she was sure. Yet what else could she have done? she argued. She did owe it to Don, after all.

When she woke it was the end of the day and the bedroom was filled with the red glow of sunset. For just a moment, she wasn't sure where she was and then as it all came back she sat up abruptly, her heart beating fast. She was on Crystal Downs cattle run; she'd been sleeping under Ryan Langton's roof. Don had gone; she was going to have to get dressed and see what could be arranged about the car. Gene had said something about Ryan and the boys—whoever they were—being out at the cattle camp all day, so she'd have to talk to Ryan tonight. That was, if he hadn't gone already.

She heard pattering footsteps, the sound of a child's voice, and a moment later the door was opened a fraction and she blinked with shock as Ryan's face appeared.

"You're awake, are you?" He pushed the door wide open and came into the room, and any protest she might have made was stifled when she saw he was carrying a small child, a little dark-haired girl in pink pyjamas, her arms affectionately round his neck, her small fair face looking incongruously delicate against his darkness.

"This is Belle. She missed you this morning and she wants to say hello before she goes downstairs to have her tea. Isn't that the idea, Belle?"

"Yes. And this is Missie," Belle said holding out the rag doll that she had clutched under one arm.

"Hello, Belle." Ashleigh sat up. She wondered who on earth the child belonged to. Ryan? Don had mentioned that he'd been married before, but she'd had the impression he'd lost his wife years ago. And hadn't Don said he wanted someone to carry on the property?

But of course, this was a girl. . . . "What are you going to have for your tea?" she heard herself asking.

"A soft—boiled—*egg*," Belle said emphatically. "Joshie chased the chooks away and we found—Oh, a lot of eggs! That's what I did this morning when you were here. You can have one too if you like. Are you sick?"

"No, I was only sleepy," Ashleigh said, charmed by the natural way the child spoke. "I'm going to get up now."

Ryan stooped and set Belle down on her slippered feet. "You run along now, sweetheart. That egg won't be soft if you stay here exchanging the time of day much longer."

"And I won't like that, will I?" Belle remarked.

She scampered off, and Ashleigh, suddenly aware of her thin pyjamas, pulled the sheet up to her chin and looked at Ryan warily. Wasn't he going to run off too? Or had he come to tell her that Charlie had fetched the car from Little Valley and mended the hole in the sump? And that she, Ashleigh Stevens, could get up and pack her bag (though actually she hadn't yet unpacked it) and be on her way. Well, she wasn't going to be in that, she thought determinedly. She could find her way to the front gate, or even to Kununurra, by daylight, if she put her mind to it, but not in the dark.

"What do you want?" she demanded.

He didn't answer, but moved across the room and sat down on the edge of the bed and looked at her steadily. Now that Belle had gone his expression had changed— drastically. She looked back at him, willing herself not to turn to jelly, but knowing it was a losing battle. Oh, how could she be so weak, so lacking in pride, she thought, agonised. She longed to pull up the sheet and hide her face so he couldn't read what was in it.

"For heaven's sake," he said after a moment, "stop

looking at me that way with those great black eyes. What on earth's going on in your mind?"

As if he didn't know! She blushed furiously and stammered out the first thing that came into her head.

"That little girl—Belle. Who is she?"

He raised one dark eyebrow. "That's Gene's kid. A little charmer, isn't she?"

"Yes, she's sweet," Ashleigh said weakly. Of course! Gene Fleming! His sister was married. "Do they—does Gene's husband live here too?"

"My sister's a widow. Her husband died a year ago in Perth. That's why she's come back home."

"Oh, I'm sorry," she exclaimed, and then because she didn't know what else to say, "I'd better get dressed, hadn't I?"

"Why not? You're certainly looking better. Maybe you aren't due for a dose of flu after all. . . . But before I leave you to it, I'd like to know if there's anyone you want informed of your whereabouts."

Quite definitely not, Ashleigh thought. If Walter and Esme knew that Laura had been left behind at Port Hedland and that she'd gone on alone with Don, Walter would be out here like a shot to fetch her back home. And that was the last thing Ashleigh wanted. What's more, Walter would go right out of his mind if he knew she'd been left in charge of Don's car and was going to be responsible for getting it to Kununurra.

"There's no one I want informed," she said positively. "Don knows where I am."

His eyes narrowed. "And he's the only one who matters, is he?"

"Yes. You don't need to contact anyone on my behalf, thank you." She said it stubbornly, and didn't care what he made of it.

He was certainly making something of it, but she hadn't the remotest idea what it was. His eyes were roaming over her in a slow and studied kind of way, and by now she'd forgotten to hang onto the sheet and the top of her pyjamas was showing. They were fine soft cotton pyjamas, palest peach with a lace and ribbon trim, not fussy, but very very pretty. *Her* style of pyjamas. And expensive, of course.

His eyes came back to her face and he said slowly, "You're a decidedly exotic dish, Miss Stevens—with your fruit-salad clothes and your eyes like blackberries and your skin like clotted cream. You come from a well-heeled family, don't you? So what the devil are you up to? Are you by any chance running away with Don Harris?"

"No, I'm not," she said and crimsoned. Because in a way she was running away with Don Harris—though not necessarily in the way Ryan Langton meant. She had yet to work out her feelings for him, as she'd just begun to realise, but she was definitely not going back to Perth. But that was her own business, so she changed the subject.

"Has your mechanic been out to see the car yet?"

"No he hasn't, Miss Stevens. We don't run a garage service on Crystal Springs for travellers who break down through their own stupidity. What's more, you'll probably have to get a spare part sent out from Kununurra or Wyndham—wherever you can get it for that make of car. Your boyfriend apparently forgot about that, didn't he? Is he always so good at passing the buck?"

Ashleigh stared at him angrily. "He's not passing the buck. He's sick. You can't expect him to think about everything."

"Can't I? You don't know me, Miss Stevens. I expect a hell of a lot from all sorts of people in all sorts of conditions."

And what did he expect of her? she wondered. That

she'd lean on him? Oh, she could see his point about careless travellers making a nuisance of themselves, but he could be a little more civil about it. At all events, she'd make the arrangements herself. She'd order the spare part, see the mechanic, and she'd be out of here so fast he'd only see her dust.

He was looking at her quizzically and she told him coolly, "I'll do my best to get out of your hair without bothering you."

He nodded. "You do that, Ashleigh. Unfortunately you're going to be stuck here longer than you think and you're not going to find it all pleasure."

Again his eyes went to her pyjama top. Or was he looking at something else? she wondered suddenly, and pulled up the sheet sharply. This fine cotton was very revealing, when she came to think about it.

"And now you can tell me about your parents, whom you don't want to contact," he said crisply.

"They're dead," Ashleigh said, and saw his eyes flicker. That had shocked him, and she felt a little ashamed of herself. "I live with my aunt and uncle," she admitted. "They know where I am and with whom." She stared straight at him. That was a lie; Walter and Esme believed she was on her way to Darwin with Laura and Don.

"I find that hard to believe, unless they have spies all over the place," he said ironically. "They can't possibly know you're here in this bedroom. With a man." He fished in his pocket and brought out cigarettes, then looked at the packet absently and put it away again. "I think you'd better give me their telephone number and I'll see they're kept informed as to where you are."

"No thank you," she said. She was still quivering from his reference to her being in this bedroom with a man. "I'll contact them myself when I know what's happening."

He looked at her levelly, a look that made her feel he could see right into her mind, and further than that. "I can tell you right now what's happening, Ashleigh. While you've been asleep I've been in touch with Kununurra—"

"About the spare part?" she put in quickly and was chagrined when he ignored the question completely.

"Don's being flown to Darwin tomorrow," he continued, as if she hadn't spoken. "The knee-cap's broken, as we suspected, and will have to be operated on. He'll have to stay in hospital for about ten days, and after that he's going to be wearing plaster for some time and learning to use crutches. Does that put you sufficiently in the picture?"

Ashleigh swallowed, her colour fading. Did he mean Don was going to be a cripple? That he wouldn't ever again be able to do the sort of work he liked doing? That he wouldn't be able to take over the safari tours?

He read her mind—not for the first time, she thought —and said with a crooked smile, "Don't get me wrong. I'm sure the knee will mend, and he'll eventually be able to take up where he left off. But it's going to take time, and one thing stands out as plain as a scrub turkey in a henhouse. He won't be going on any safari tours for quite a while." He let her digest that and then asked briskly, "What kind of a job did you leave behind you in Perth—if any?"

*If any,* she thought, stung. That meant he thought she was useless as well as everything else.

"I was personal secretary to the director of a mining company, as it happens," she said deliberately. And that was something *he* could digest, she thought with satisfaction. She didn't have to tell him that the director was her uncle or that it had been Esme's idea that she should work for him.

"You'll learn something about the business world,"

Esme had said. "Meet the right sort of people, which you wouldn't do if you worked in a crafts shop, like Laura."

In actual fact, her uncle had a very competent secretary and Ashleigh had often thought she was little more than a nuisance. She typed letters, made occasional phone calls out but didn't take those coming in except when Anna was out at lunch. Other than that she fixed the flowers, tidied up, got in the way generally, and sometimes went with Walter to business luncheons—and hated it. Could anyone wonder she'd grabbed at the chance to escape and go north, where she could build a life of her own?

"And you gave that up to come to the tropics," Ryan said studying her as intently as if she'd suddenly sprouted eight arms and an extra head, she thought stifling a laugh.

"Yes."

"I won't ask you if your aunt and uncle approve. I'm damned sure they don't. One has only to look at your clothes—even those pyjamas or nightgown or whatever it is you're wearing—to know the sort of thing you've been brought up to want from life. Do you think you're likely to get it here—or in Darwin?"

"You'd be surprised," she said dryly. And he would be, too, she thought. He hadn't the least idea what she wanted from life, no matter how she'd been brought up by Esme and Walter. That could be because she was her mother's daughter, and her mother had wanted adventure. She didn't place all that much value on money and appearances when it came to happiness. These pyjamas, her suitcase full of pretty and expensive clothes, she'd give them all up on the spot in exchange for love.

She'd been staring at Ryan Langton blankly as these thoughts flashed through her mind, and she blinked when he said, "Well, I suppose it's up to you what you do with your life. I'll leave you to dress. There's no hurry. Dinner won't be ready until after Belle's been put to bed."

He got up from the bed and crossed to the door, then paused to tell her sardonically, "Don't go to too much trouble with your dress, will you? It's not a big occasion. We're not celebrating anything."

Ashleigh coloured. He was snubbing her, emphasising the fact that she was imposing on him. She bit back a retort and gave vent to her feelings by pulling a face at his back as he left the room.

At least Gene was friendly and ready to hand out a little country hospitality, she reflected as she got out of bed. She'd get dressed quickly and go downstairs and see if she could help in the kitchen. She'd be quite safe from Ryan there, at any rate.

How wrong can you be? she thought half an hour later. Because in the kitchen, Ryan was dealing with the dinner and Gene was nowhere to be seen.

Ashleigh hovered in the doorway, not nearly so certain about offering to help him as she had been of helping his sister.

"Surprised, Miss Stevens?" His blue eyes were amused, and she blushed. "Gene's telling Belle a story. I told you there was no hurry."

So what did she do now, she wondered? Somehow she didn't think he needed any help. A big, stemmed bowl of clear glass held salad vegetables, and on a counter with an ivory matte finish there were steaks ready to grill. The kitchen was old-fashioned in that it was big, but it was modern in its equipment: fridge and freezer, an electric stove, and another that ran off cylindered gas. There were light pine cupboards, plenty of bench space, a big ceiling fan, and windows opening onto a narrow verandah, shaded by peppercorn trees.

An open door on the far side of the room gave a glimpse into a formal dining room, while the door she'd come in by, from the hallway, led straight into a good-sized dinette area, divided from the kitchen by a long counter. The table was already laid for three, and in fact everything seemed under control.

Everything except for her heart, which raced alarmingly as she watched that . . . macho man mixing up French dressing, and sparing more than a casual glance for her as he did so, his dazzlingly blue gaze wandering interestedly over the soft simple cream dress she was wearing with a violet belt and shoes and glass earrings to match.

"I hope I'm not overdressed," she said huskily.

He raised his eyes and their glances locked. Almost, it seemed to Ashleigh, with a click.

"No, you're not overdressed. But you're just as much of a menace in the kitchen as anywhere else, and if you stand there looking at me much longer there'll be no dinner tonight."

He was joking of course, yet her heart pounded harder than ever and she almost expected him to come round the counter and seize her in his arms.

Perhaps he would have done just that if Gene hadn't joined them at that moment with the flippant remark, "You'll make some lucky girl a marvellous husband one day, Ryan."

"Don't be too sure," he quipped back, equally flippantly. "Once I have a wife to wait on me I'll put my feet up. . . . Why don't you pour our guest a drink, while she's waiting to be fed? I seem to remember her favourite tipple is orange juice, but she might like something a little more potent tonight."

"A whisky for you, anyhow," Gene said. "How about joining me in a sherry, Ashleigh?"

Yes, Ashleigh felt a sherry would help her through

dinner; or rather, that it might settle her nerves that were still tingling from the way Ryan looked at her.

Ryan disappeared immediately after dinner and Gene stacked the dishes in the sink.

"The girls will clean up in the morning. Minnie disappeared a couple of days ago to go walkabout. Heaven knows when she'll come back—she could be gone two weeks or two months—but Violet's young sister Priss is doing her bit," she remarked, as they made their way into the living room.

It was a spacious room with long glass doors opening onto the verandah. There were two comfortable-looking sofas and a variety of chairs, two coffee tables and a small round table covered with an ecru linen cloth, holding a large pot plant. Other pot plants made cool green splashes against the wall; a group of framed paintings of birds decorated another wall.

"I'm sorry Ryan's being unsociable," Gene remarked as they sat down, Ashleigh in a cushioned cane chair, Gene on one of the sofas, where she kicked off her shoes and tucked her feet under her. "He seems to have some problem on his mind. He's not usually quite so remote when he's been away for a few days."

Ashleigh thought she was probably the reason for his remoteness, but Gene would have to work that out for herself.

"He didn't get back from Broome till late last evening and I haven't had a chance to talk to him. He went out to the stock camp early this morning. I didn't expect him back for a few days actually, and then he turned up with you."

Ashleigh bit her lip. "I'm afraid I'm a nuisance." She was on the point of bringing up the subject of ordering the spare part for the car, but Gene spoke first.

"I'm enjoying your company, anyhow. But tell me

something—when you met Ryan and Debra in Broome, was anything said about them being engaged?"

Ashleigh shook her head. "We weren't talking about personal matters," she said uncomfortably. "Pearls seemed to be the main topic of conversation over dinner."

Gene sighed. "Blow! I'm just dying to know what's happening, and Ryan's not the sort of man you can put on the mat. My younger brothers are much more forthcoming about the girls they're interested in. Ryan's touchy about marriage."

She stopped abruptly and after a moment Ashleigh heard herself ask, "He was married before, wasn't he?"

"Who told you that?" Gene sounded surprised.

"Don," Ashleigh said, wishing she'd kept her mouth shut because it sounded like prying.

"Her name was Christine," Gene said after a moment. "They were both terribly young and it lasted less than a year. She died of leukaemia. I guess he's never really gotten over it. He has a very soft heart in spite of his maddeningly overbearing ways. Emotionally, I'm a whole lot tougher."

"Are you?" Ashleigh was having trouble thinking of Ryan as having a soft heart and yet when he'd come to her room this evening with Belle he'd been tender, gentle with the child.

"I want to marry again," she heard Gene say. "If I can find the right sort of man. Which I shan't do in the Kimberleys, so it will have to wait till I get back to Perth."

"When will that be?"

Gene shrugged. "When Ryan marries. I wouldn't dream of walking out on him before that. He's had so much trouble with housekeepers since mother died." She looked at Ashleigh through narrowed eyes. "It's odd, but you remind me of Christine somehow. It can't

really be your looks. Her hair was as fair as yours is
dark, and she had big grey eyes. But quite definitely
there's something."

Ashleigh was aware of a slight sense of shock. If
Ryan noticed a resemblance too, could that explain his
ambivalent attitude towards her? It was something
she'd have to think about later, though it might be
better if she forgot about Ryan Langton altogether.

She moved restlessly, and Gene said, "It's probably
just my imagination. . . . Anyhow, from the way Ryan
rushed off to Broome I'm positive he means to marry
Debra. She's been visiting here on and off for ages. My
mother used to invite her right up to when she died two
years ago. She thought she'd make an ideal wife for
Ryan, and I agree. I guess it will all work out when she
comes to visit us again, which will be soon, as she's
arranging to have a holiday. But I suppose I'm boring
you to tears with all this family talk. How do you like
the outback, anyway?"

"Oh, I like it," Ashleigh admitted cautiously. It was
curious, but it was true. She almost felt she'd been born
in the outback. She had a feeling of kinship with it; she
was fascinated. That was hardly logical, she thought
ironically, seeing she'd got lost, put Don's car out of
commission, and been very frightened by the situation
she'd landed herself in.

"Really? All the same, I hope you're not seriously
thinking of marrying that male chauvinist friend of
yours with the filthy temper."

Ashleigh felt the hot colour rush to her cheeks. Of
course she was thinking of marrying Don, and he
wasn't the way Gene supposed.

"I'm sorry you had that impression of Don," she said
stiffly. "I suppose you heard what he was saying to me
about the accident. But he did apologise afterwards,
you know."

"For being a louse," Gene said. "Yes, I heard that

too. . . . Oh well, I shouldn't be rude about him. But I don't believe in women putting up with that sort of thing from men and you really shouldn't let him blame you for what was obviously an accident."

She looked at Ashleigh as if she expected a comment from her, but Ashleigh decided on silence. She didn't want to discuss Don with anyone, or to have people offering her advice, no matter how well meant. She'd work things out for herself, and that was that.

Gene was tactful enough not to pursue the subject, and instead suggested they should see what was on TV. "At least we have that, these days," she remarked. "Thanks to InterSat 4."

Before they went upstairs to bed some time later, Ashleigh brought up the subject of Don's car. "I'll have to see the mechanic about it. How do I do that?"

Gene spread her hands and shrugged. "I think you'd better discuss it with Ryan. He's the one who employs Charlie."

Ashleigh grimaced inwardly. Discussing it with Ryan was just what she didn't want to do. Besides, when was she going to have an opportunity to discuss anything with Ryan? He'd disappeared straight after dinner, and Gene had said he'd be leaving early in the morning for the muster camp, but that she hoped he wouldn't sleep out there. Gene meant to put it to him that he and her other two brothers, Colin and David, should all come home, "seeing we have a guest," she added.

Ashleigh suspected that that very fact would keep Ryan, at least, as far away from the homestead as possible. That was the feeling he'd given her. . . .

In her room as she undressed, Ashleigh wondered where he slept and if he'd already gone to bed—and then she decided to put him out of her mind, which was easier said than done. She lay awake, thinking of nothing else. Thinking of Christine, wondering if that odd resemblance was the reason Ryan was both attracted by her and antagonistic to her; if it was of Christine he thought when he took her in his arms.

She switched her thoughts over to the problem of the car and Don. Of course she wanted to get away from here and be with him, but she was not looking forward to driving all the way to Darwin, which must be a good thousand kilometres. It really would have been better for her to have gone with Don in the plane. But he was the one who'd insisted she must stay here . . . and now look at the mess she was in! Worried sick not only about the car but also about her stupid attraction to the sexiest man in the Kimberleys. . . .

# Chapter Five

When she woke in the morning, it wasn't quite six o'clock, but she could hear someone moving about. A door was shut quietly and footsteps passed her room and went down the stairs—a man's footsteps. So it was Ryan. He must be going out to the stock camp.

She sat up in the bed, pushing her hair back from her cheeks. She had to see him before he disappeared—maybe for days—to ask him about seeing that mechanic of his. She had to get away from here, and yet she was aware of a strong feeling of reluctance. The trouble was, she was getting obsessed by Ryan Langton, and there was no future in that. He was in the process of getting engaged to another woman. And it was sheer idiocy to keep dwelling on their encounters; to imagine she meant anything at all to him, other than reminding him in some way of the girl he'd once loved, Ashleigh reflected with a feeling of bitterness.

So it seemed that Ashleigh Stevens had better smarten herself up and get out of here fast, in which case, she was going to pester Ryan Langton until she got something done about that car.

She got resolutely out of bed, shrugged into her robe—hyacinth blue, frilled, and very very feminine—and after making a quick visit to the bathroom and running a comb through her glossy dark hair, she made her way down the stairs.

In the kitchen, she found Ryan, efficiently preparing a breakfast of steak and eggs for himself.

"You're up early," he greeted her as she appeared in the dinette. "I hope you're not going to ask me to take you out to the stock camp with me. I've far too much on my mind to have city girls gawping around and asking questions and distracting everyone."

"Thank you for making your feelings so plain," she flared, taken aback by his attack. "But believe it or not I'm not the slightest bit interested in gawping around anywhere in your vicinity, Mr. Langton."

"No?" He turned back to the stove to attend to his sizzling steak and eggs, then flicked her an enigmatic blue glance over his shoulder so that she thought furiously, I'm gawping around now.

"What is it you're after, then?" He'd swung round and his gaze trailed down her slender figure, its curves revealed by the soft material of her robe. "Or did you come down solely to let me get an eyeful of your provoking loveliness in your bedroom gear?"

Ashleigh could have screamed. Imagine thinking she was attracted by a man like that! Gene talked about Don's bad temper, his chauvinism, but Ryan Langton was ruder and more infuriating than any man she'd ever met.

"I merely wanted to ask you where I can contact your mechanic to ask him to go and take a look at Don's car," she said through her teeth. "Since I gather you'll be out for the day—or even longer—it seemed sense to see you before you left and consult you about what I wanted to do."

"Forget it," he said flatly. "Charlie's out at the stock camp, in any case." He dished up his steak and eggs, poured himself a cup of coffee, and sat down at the table facing her. "Don't get the idea I'm uncooperative, but nothing can be done until that spare part's flown in on the mail-plane. I'll order whatever's needed, but it won't be here for another five days and only then if you're lucky. I'm afraid you're going to have to sit and twiddle your thumbs."

He looked up and their eyes met as he finished and that electric spark flashed between them so that Ashleigh went weak at the knees. It seemed incredible that he could be talking to her the way he was and that there was still that indefinable something between them that was impossible to deny. He was just as much aware of it as she was. She was certain of it because of the suddenness with which he stopped looking at her.

"You'd better run off back to bed. Get some more beauty sleep. Not that you need it," he added and frowned as if he hadn't meant to say that. "Forget about Don's car for awhile."

"How can I?" she flashed. She wanted to make him look at her again, she wanted it with a fierceness that was like hunger, and she leaned against the door frame, her nerves quivering. Thoughts of living here forever, of getting his breakfast in the mornings, of going out to the stock camp with him, of waiting for him to come home to dinner at night, of going upstairs with him to bed, chased each other through her mind. She brushed them aside and went on angrily. "Do you think I enjoy being stuck here helpless when Don's in hospital and all our plans are in such a muddle? I know I'm imposing on you—that you hate having me here—"

"Is that what you think?" He looked at her briefly

through lashes that were thick and dark, his mouth curving slightly. "Admittedly I wouldn't have invited you to stay, but my sister did, and you're here now, for better or for worse. Unfortunately for you, in the Kimberleys you can't have what you want just by asking for it. Some things take time." He gave her a measuring look, then attacked his breakfast again. "Ask Gene to take you out in the car today. You ought to see some of our beauty spots before you go. I suggest the Crystal Pool. You can take a swim there. And have a game of tennis this evening."

"I don't want to swim or play tennis," she said coolly. "All I want is to get away."

"Then be sure I'll see what I can do on your behalf," he snapped. "We might hear of someone driving over from Kununurra or Wyndham. In which case, you could be out of here even before I come back from the stock camp. Would that suit you?"

"Yes, it would," she said tightly.

"Right."

The curt way he said it sounded like dismissal and she accepted it as such. She was halfway across the hall when she heard him behind her. He took hold of her arm roughly and spun her round towards him, then held her a foot away from him, his eyes flashing blue fire for an instant before he kissed her.

"That's for good bye," he said huskily. He held her arms hard and their eyes met. "You really shouldn't do it, Ashleigh."

"Do what?" she asked unsteadily.

His mouth twisted. "Tempt me."

She shook her head. "I don't."

"Oh yes, you do. Every time I see you in your pretty pastel colours and you fix those dark velvet eyes on me. I've never met a girl so intent on starting a stampede."

He wound his arms around her and crushed her to

him again, and she closed her eyes and heard him mutter as his mouth brushed against hers, "If I didn't have an appointment with a helicopter in an hour's time, I'd take you upstairs to bed."

His lips moved passionately over hers and she felt herself trembling with desire for him, and knew he felt it too. And she didn't care. Nothing except the pressure of his body against hers, the soft seductive demands of his mouth—his closeness to her, his warmth, his physical reality—seemed to matter any more, and she moulded herself to his hardness and wished to the depths of her soul that he didn't have an appointment with a helicopter—that the whole day was theirs to make love.

"Ryan." She moved her mouth fractionally from his to whisper his name and look up into his eyes, her own hiding nothing.

He gave a smothered exclamation and pulled her arms from around his neck.

"Let's not get carried away," he said thickly. "Better thank your lucky stars I do have an appointment." His eyes held hers fiercely and unreadably, and then abruptly he turned on his heel and went back to his breakfast.

She was crazy and she knew it, but she started to run after him, and had almost reached the door when she heard the sound of voices in the kitchen. The house-girls. She stopped, her heart thumping, and then fled back across the hall and up the stairs to her bedroom, where she flung herself face down on the bed.

Her mind went completely blank and it seemed a lifetime passed before someone knocked softly on the door. Ryan, was her instant thought, and she sat up in confusion, wondering what he wanted.

But of course it wasn't Ryan. It was one of the house-girls, a pretty dark-skinned aboriginal girl in a pink cotton dress, bringing her a cup of tea, setting it down on the bedside table with a shy smile.

"Ryan said you might like this."

Ashleigh smiled and said thank you and the girl went silently away.

A cup of tea. Yes—she could do with it. She wondered, as she drank the hot sweet liquid, if it had been an understanding gesture on Ryan's part, or whether it was more likely to be a touch of irony.

She was full of nerves when she came downstairs later on. She breakfasted with Gene and Belle, and the child's chatter fortunately cut conversation to a minimum. Afterwards, the house-girls—Violet, who'd brought the cup of tea, and Priss, younger and shyer—came in to clear up and to have Gene tell them what she wanted done about the homestead. When that had been dealt with, Gene took her to meet Selma Gray, who lived in one of the attractive bungalows beyond the homestead garden. She was the mechanic's wife, and the mother of three children: Adam who was ten; Paula, seven; and little Josh, who was Belle's playmate. They were on the verandah, where the two older children were doing their school lessons, and Gene collected Josh, so that he and Belle could play together.

"Do you hear that helicopter?" Adam asked as they were leaving. "I asked Mr. Langton if I could go up in it, but Mum won't let me."

"I should think not," his mother said. She was a small, pretty woman in her early thirties, her skin hardened by the tropical sun, but her eyes gentle. "You have school lessons to do, and besides, you'd only make a nuisance of yourself."

Adam grimaced. "No I wouldn't. Mr. Langton likes kids, anyhow. You just think it's dangerous or something."

"Well, it's not exactly safe," Selma said. "And I

don't like the idea of you going in the helicopter when they're mustering cattle out of the scrub."

"It'd be exciting," Adam protested. "Dad doesn't think it's dangerous. He'd have let me go out to the camp with him this morning if you hadn't gone on about school work."

"That's enough, son," his mother said briskly, and Adam went disconsolately back to join Paula, who was poring frowningly over her school books.

So that was what Ryan had meant when he said he had an appointment with a helicopter, Ashleigh reflected as she and Gene walked back to the homestead garden. The two small children walked ahead of them. Josh carried his ginger kitten, Pumpkin; Belle, her doll Missie. And, Ashleigh recalled, Charlie, the mechanic, was out there at the camp as well.

A few questions elicited the further information that the stock camp was not far from Little Valley, and in no time the idea of going out there had taken root in Ashleigh's mind. She knew it wasn't solely because of the car that she wanted to get out there. She was interested in going to the cattle camp as well. Anyone would be, she told herself and hastily pushed aside the mental image of Ryan that kept floating tantalisingly and aggravatingly before her eyes. It really was important to have Charlie look at the car, and she didn't altogether trust Ryan. He wasn't going to put himself out for travellers who broke down on his cattle run. She suspected that no spare part might be needed after all, in which case she'd be able to set off for Darwin that much sooner. . . . which, if she were honest with herself, she didn't in the least want to do. In her heart, she knew very well she was looking for an excuse to get out to the stock camp, to gawp around in Ryan's vicinity. So perhaps she'd better forget it, she decided reluctantly.

She didn't, of course. When lunch was over and

Gene asked what she'd like to do, she said promptly that she'd like to see Charlie and try to hurry up the repairs to the car.

"I know Ryan's busy, and I do feel worried about Don. If he's going to be laid up in hospital and then have his leg in plaster, I ought to be around to help. But I suppose I'm nuisance enough staying here, without asking you to go out of your way to humour my whims."

"Oh you're not a nuisance, don't be so silly," Gene said quickly. "Surely you know I'm enjoying having you here. . . . And if you want to see Charlie, then okay. Put on some old clothes, get your hat and your sun-glasses, and away we'll go. I guess I know how you feel—all on edge, though I'm sure you could safely leave everything to Ryan. Still, it will be nice for you to meet David and Colin. And maybe when they see what sort of a visitor we have," she added with a wicked smile, "they'll decide to come home and be civilised for awhile, instead of sleeping out in their horrid little mosquito-proof tents."

In half an hour they were in the Mini Moke and on their way, with Belle sitting in the back seat. Ashleigh had done her best about dress, but she didn't have any old clothes with her, because she wasn't really an old clothes sort of girl. She wore pale cinnamon pants and a lime green sleeveless top; unfortunately her hat was unwearable.

They left the home paddock and drove across endless acres of long drying grass, heading towards hazy violet ranges that hovered just above the horizon, seeming to be separated from it by a strip of shimmering water. But the water didn't exist, Ashleigh soon discovered. It was a mirage.

They must have come this way back from Little Valley, but at that time she'd been too disturbed to take much interest in her surroundings. Now it was different, and she was fascinated by the strawlike grasses, the blue of wild kapok, the white trunks of the snappy gums. The sky was pale and clear, washed in here and there with streaky water-colour clouds, and her eyes dwelt lingeringly on the creamy foam of blossom on the bloodwoods, the long silvery leaves of the grevilleas, then followed a flock of white corellas as they went wheeling out into the emptiness.

The country in the ranges was like the valley where she and Don had been stranded. Deep pools of water reflected the blue of the sky, and cattle rested on the sandy ground in the shade of the kajeputs. From somewhere far off came the sound of a helicopter roaring, and Belle in the back of the Moke squeaked out excitedly, "That's Uncle Ryan, isn't it, Mummy?"

Uncle Ryan! Ashleigh had to make a mental adjustment to transform the man she knew into "Uncle Ryan."

"Does he fly the 'copter?" she queried, feeling a little shiver pass through her, because it must be at least a slightly dangerous undertaking.

Gene shook her head. She looked hot and Ashleigh suspected she wasn't enjoying driving out here very much and felt guilty at having asked her to do so.

"He does have a pilot's licence, but he uses a helicopter mustering service. The outfit provides a pilot, and he goes up to direct operations. They keep in contact with the ground party by radio, and as the cattle are hunted out, the stockmen take them over and yard them for drafting and branding. They're getting some cattle together for sale. They'll be droved to the loading yards down by the road in a few days' time, I expect." She sent Ashleigh a mocking glance. "Not that I know a great deal about it. I'm just not the outdoor type. I'm very happy to leave Crystal Downs to my brothers. I don't own a square inch of it, you know. My parents left me some money instead."

By now they'd reached the muster camp, and as Gene pulled up in the shade of trees, the helicopter rattled overhead, then swooped down over the scrub-covered slopes, its shadow flying along as the cattle came racing ahead of it. The siren honked, jabirus and hawks scattered, and on the ground dust rose and stock-whips cracked.

The two women sat in the car, their eyes screwed up, watching. Most of the stockmen were aborigines, but the man who came riding up to the Land Rover presently was obviously one of Gene's brothers—young, good-looking, wearing a checked shirt and a wide-brimmed hat and tight cord trousers. His eyes were on Ashleigh, who felt embarrassed about her inappropriate get-up. She'd intended to stock up on country gear when she was in Darwin, as Esme would have suspected she was up to something if she'd done so in Perth. So it was too bad she was now stranded on a cattle station and unable to produce clothes that would make her melt into the background.

"This is David," Gene said. "My youngest brother."

"The pick of the bunch," David put in with a boyish laugh that showed his white teeth. He was more like his sister than Ryan, fair-haired and blue-eyed, tallish, bursting with good health. "And you're Ashleigh Stevens, the latest casualty on Crystal Downs. I'd have been first on the scene to answer your smoke signal, but the boss said no."

Ashleigh blushed at the way he was looking at her and met his blue eyes directly as he went on.

"I hope you came out here today specifically to make my acquaintance, that my loving sister told you what a prize I am." He stooped to kiss Belle, who'd clambered out of the car, and Ashleigh found that he had the same tender loving air as Ryan had when it came to children.

Ashleigh too had gotten out of the car, but Gene stayed where she was, and Ashleigh looked around her searchingly. "Actually I came to see Charlie," she told David. "Is he anywhere around?"

"Sure. Come along with me and we'll rustle him up. . . . Are you coming, Genie?"

"No thanks. I can collect all the dust and flies I need right here where I am."

"Lazy," David said and sent Ashleigh another admiring glance. "If I'd known you were *that* sort of visitor I wouldn't have been sleeping out here in the bush the last couple of nights. It's the home paddock for me tonight." He took her arm in a friendly way and a moment later indicated a slightly overweight man of about forty who was inspecting the engine of a rather ancient car. "This is Charlie, the world's greatest mechanic. . . . Someone to speak to you, Charlie. . . . Here, what'll I do with this kid?" he asked, smiling down at Belle, who was hopping around in the vicinity. "Want to come for a ride with me, Belle?"

Belle wrinkled her nose, in much the same way her mother did. "No thank you—I don't like the smell of horses. Mummy's brought a book for me to read in the car."

"Then I'll take you back, you little squib. I'll see you later, Ashleigh. Right?"

"Yes." Ashleigh had the feeling she need only give the smallest sign and David would be all over her like a rash. Certainly he was nice, but she wasn't interested. She turned her attention to Charlie, who was looking at her speculatively.

"Mr. Gray—"

"Oh call me 'Charlie,'" he protested before she could go on.

"Charlie. I wondered if you could possibly drive out to the Little Valley and take a look at—at my car. There's supposed to be a hole in the sump, and I'm very anxious to get it fixed up so I can get to Darwin."

"Then hop in the car," he said promptly. "Anything to oblige a lady."

He smiled laconically and Ashleigh nearly fell over. She couldn't believe her luck. They were going out this very minute! She only hoped Ryan wouldn't turn up and put a stop to it.

She looked around guiltily, but Ryan was up in the helicopter; even if he should happen to see what was happening, there was nothing he could do about it.

In seconds she was sitting beside Charlie in the old car and they were careering through the dust away from the camp and the bellowing cattle. Ashleigh waved cheerfully to Gene as they passed; then, sobering down, she remarked, "It's very good of you to take all this trouble for me, Charlie. I hope there won't be any bother about it later on."

He raised an eyebrow. "Bother? Good Lord, no! The boss told me first thing this morning to get out there as soon as I had a chance, but my old bomb's been playing up and I had to get that fixed first. I'd have been gone if you'd turned up five minutes later, so you're in luck."

Ashleigh grimaced. So she wasn't doing something tricky behind Ryan's back in having Charlie drive out to take a look at the car! Ryan had actually asked his mechanic to take a look at it.

Charlie offered her a cigarette, then lit one for himself when she shook her head. Ashleigh told him she'd met Selma and the children, then listened as he talked proudly about Adam.

"He's a great little kid, game enough for anything. But I don't want him to take up stock-work. Want him to get a good education, use his brains. Be different if I were a cattleman, but I'm a mechanic. Trouble is, once you get hooked on this part of the world, you don't want to leave it."

His drawling, laconic voice was a little hard to follow, but Ashleigh listened interestedly until at last they reached the place where the car was stranded. While Charlie examined it, she looked around her. Curiously, the accident seemed to have happened ages ago, in another lifetime. Now she couldn't even remember folding up the sleeping bags and stowing them away in the car. But she must have done that and a whole lot more, because there was nothing lying about.

Charlie came back soon, a wry expression on his face. "You certainly knocked a hole in that sump, Ashleigh—big enough to let a crocodile crawl inside. Engine seized up too. . . . I'll have to tow the car back to the homestead when I come."

"Will you be able to fix it?" she asked hopefully, and he grunted out a laugh.

"Not until we can get what I'll need brought out on the mail-plane. Don't you worry, though. We'll have it back on the road just as fast as ever we can."

So she wouldn't be out of here by tomorrow, she reflected, and knew she wasn't sorry. She didn't want to leave Crystal Downs yet, or Ryan either, if she were honest. He puzzled her, he was rude, yet there was still that irresistible attraction, and wherever it led, even if it was to nowhere, she was mesmerised by it. She was like a mermaid being lured to her doom by a cattleman, she thought ridiculously, and laughed inwardly at the thought.

Back at the camp, the first thing she noticed was that Gene's Mini Moke was nowhere to be seen. Charlie let her out of the car and she stood looking around her bewilderedly.

"Where's Gene?" she asked David, who appeared a few minutes later out of a cloud of dust that was a smoky pink as the sun began to go down.

"Gone back to the homestead. Belle was playing up—that kid hasn't got used to cattle yet. . . . But don't worry, I promised I'd take you home. I'll only be five minutes."

Ashleigh looked around quickly and there was not a sign of Ryan, though she hadn't heard the 'copter for some time. She was dismayed at the thought of coming all this way and not even seeing him. "I hope it's not putting you out," she said doubtfully.

David widened his eyes. "Ashleigh, I'm delighted to be put out by someone as delectable as you." He turned slightly as another man came to join them. "You haven't met Colin yet, have you? Don't be taken in by anything he says to you. He has a girl in Katherine and the vital question is about to be popped at any minute now. Colin, meet Ashleigh Stevens and take note that I saw her first."

Colin, who was very like his brother (they were all fair except Ryan), grinned. "Hi, Ashleigh. Too bad for me that one woman at a time is all I can handle. Otherwise young David would have to watch out. Are you enjoying yourself at Crystal Downs?"

"Very much—in the little time I've been here."

"Things will warm up once we get the cattle on the road," he promised. "We'll all be home then, so get ready for the invasion."

Ashleigh wondered if she'd still be there and hoped a little that she would. She liked the two younger Langton boys. They were so uncomplicated, so full of good humour and laughter. So why in heaven's name did she have to be enthralled by the other one—the one who was different, the one who had a heart like a stone though sex oozed out of him at every pore? She shuddered away from her own thoughts. This wasn't the way Ashleigh Stevens was accustomed to thinking.

She glanced over Colin's shoulder—she didn't know why, but something seemed to make her look. And— she might have guessed it—there was Ryan striding towards them, the red light of sunset on his face, looking taller, broader, more overwhelmingly masculine than ever. She winced at the emotions that washed over her in a wave, even though he was glaring at her.

"Still here, Ashleigh Stevens?" he said tightly. "I hope you're not planning to stay at the camp overnight." His eyes raked over her, a curious expression in them: half contempt, half something else. And she knew what that something else was. It was the way a man looks at a woman who attracts him sexually, and it made her feel weak all over again. She pulled her sun-glasses from her pocket and put them on as if to shield herself from something.

"No, I'm not planning to stay overnight," she began unevenly, and at the same moment David said, "Calm down, Ryan. There aren't going to be any riots in the camp. I'm taking Ashleigh home."

Ryan sent him a frowning look. "I'm afraid you're not. You're staying right here. I've arranged for Roger to bring the helicopter out again first thing in the A.M. There's a whole mob of cattle still in the scrub, and I want you to go up and direct operations. You can do with some experience in that field. . . . I'll see Ashleigh gets home."

Ashleigh saw the quick look the two younger brothers exchanged, but she doubted whether Ryan did. He was already moving off, merely saying over his shoulder, "Hang around, Miss Stevens. I'll be with you in a few minutes."

Ashleigh looked at David. "I'm sorry."

"Not as sorry as I am," David grimaced. "And I thought I saw you first! Oh well, stay out of mischief till we meet again, won't you?" He gave her a speculative look.

Meaning what? she wondered. She had half a mind to tell him that she knew all about Debra. Yet knowing all about Debra didn't seem to keep her out of mischief.

Colin raised his hand in salute and he and David moved away, and she leaned against the smooth white trunk of a nearby tree and watched what was going on. Work for the day had ceased, and the brilliantly coloured clouds that had swarmed across the sky were fast dispersing, leaving it a clear, glowing red. Dust hovered over the mob of restless cattle that had been mustered, and three aboriginal stockmen rode slowly around on the outskirts. Dinner was in preparation—she could smell it cooking—and she supposed all the men, David and Colin included, would be having a clean-up, getting ready for their meal. It was an all-male world, and nothing would have induced her to even think of camping out here unless Gene had been staying too, or she'd been invited. Or unless she were married to one of the Langtons, she finished the thought, and found an odd attraction in it.

It appeared that David was the only Langton who was available, and Ryan was not encouraging his brother to take an interest in Ashleigh Stevens, that was for sure. She felt goose pimples on her skin when she thought of the way she reacted to Ryan. He had only to look at her, to touch her, and everything flew out of her mind. There were just herself and him, alone in the world. As for how he felt about her . . . that was something she couldn't fathom.

"Come along, Ashleigh." Ryan had materialised, and took hold of her arm firmly, to steer her over to his car. Instantly, a tremor ran along her nerves. She simply couldn't help it and it was maddening. She shook her arm free then stumbled on the rough ground and felt a fool.

"I thought you were going to stay out at the camp for the next few nights," she remarked when they were in the car and driving away from the camp.

"So I was," he said flatly.

"Then why did you change your plans?"

He didn't answer for a moment, and then he said slowly, "I don't know how you hope I'm going to answer that question, Ashleigh, but I changed my plans quite simply because someone has to take you back to the homestead, and no one else is available." He turned his head and looked at her sardonically. "Why didn't you go back home with Gene?"

Why? Because Gene had vanished while she was away with Charlie. But she wasn't going to tell him that and lay the blame on Gene.

"Oh, I thought someone would take me home," she said carelessly.

"How right you were," he agreed. "And by the way, if you have ideas of fascinating my young brother, I'm sure you'll have no trouble at all. Love, like the dark, comes quickly in the outback—if that thought gives you any satisfaction."

Antagonism flared up in her. "I came out to see Charlie, not to fascinate anyone," she retorted.

"Why in the world would you want to see Charlie? To find out if I was holding out on you? I hope you're satisfied that I've been playing it perfectly straight."

"More or less," she said stiffly, and silence fell between them. Ashleigh could feel his irritation with her almost tangibly, and if she imagined there was something else mixed with it, she was probably fooling herself. He'd played with her, stirred her, and now she was no more than a nuisance. . . .

# Chapter Six

Ryan was right about the dark, she reflected presently. It did come quickly—the eerie, starry, outback night. She and Ryan seemed to be in the middle of nowhere, and she looked out at the fantastic starlit wilderness; at the dark shapes of birds, or were they fruit bats? against the velvet of the sky; at the white trunks of trees; the grass hummocks; the weird termite mounds —all emerging briefly in a whirl of fleeting shadows in the headlights of the car.

Though at first she'd been acutely and sensitively conscious of Ryan's physical presence, she gradually relaxed completely. This was where she wanted to be, where she belonged. Right here, she thought, and knew that "right here" included being at Ryan's side. But when he spoke abruptly out of the darkness, she discovered his mind was travelling a very different path from hers.

"I insisted that David should stay at the camp tonight because he has to learn to take his responsibilities seriously. I've been running this cattle station ever since my father died eleven years ago when I was twenty-two, the same age as David is now. I've been a little too easy-going with my young brothers, and it doesn't do. . . . However, I daresay you thought me dictatorial just now."

Ashleigh murmured something unintelligible. She had thought him that, but she knew that she'd far sooner be here with him than with David, so why should she care?

"We own another cattle run in the back country," Ryan went on. "My two brothers are to take it over in a few months' time, when the manager's term is up. It's not good country. We breed cattle there and fatten them up on the Mitchell grass pasture here. But like any cattle run, it needs good management to make it work. If David took you back home tonight, I know damned well he wouldn't turn up at the stock camp at all tomorrow, and that's not good enough. I daresay he's keen to find himself a wife, but he can do it in his spare time."

"I see," Ashleigh said flushing. "I know now why you said I'd have no trouble fascinating him."

He changed the subject abruptly. "What did Charlie tell you about the car?"

"It's the sump," she said. "He's promised to fix it as soon as he can."

"You're in a hurry to get to Darwin, are you?"

"Yes of course," she said firmly and glanced at him from under her lashes.

He drove on for a couple of minutes, then suddenly put his foot on the brake so that the car pulled up with a jerk. Ashleigh's heart beat feverishly.

She'd turned towards him without even being aware of it the minute his hands left the wheel, and in less than a second their mouths were clinging. She responded to his kisses passionately, feeling the hardness of his chest against her body as his tongue explored her mouth; melting against him helplessly, surrendering completely to the sensations his love-making induced.

Then with a groan he let her go. "I don't know why the hell I took it on myself to drive you back to the homestead, Ashleigh Stevens. I should have handed you over to my brother."

"Then . . . why didn't you?" she asked unevenly, sure she knew why—that it was because of this desperate, inescapable attraction between them. "Isn't he . . . trustworthy?"

"Oh yes," he said cynically. "David's all of that. But are you?"

Ashleigh thought she was. She was inclined to think she could trust herself with any man alive—except with Ryan Langton, and at this very minute, what she wanted most was for him to go on making love to her.

But he didn't. He drove on—fast in spite of the darkness, though he probably knew all these thousands of acres of his like the back of his hand. In no time at all, the glimmer of lights appeared, and then they'd pulled up outside the homestead. The door opened and Gene came onto the verandah as though she'd been waiting for them.

"Oh, it's you, Ryan!" she exclaimed in surprise. "I asked David to bring Ashleigh home."

Ryan got out of the car, flung open Ashleigh's door, then slammed it shut after she'd emerged.

"So it was your idea, was it? Well, David has more important things to do with his time than taxiing female visitors around." He walked past her and took the steps to the verandah two at a time, heedless of whether Ashleigh was coming or not. "There are times when you're just so damned interfering it isn't funny, Gene. Doesn't it ever occur to you that running the stock camp is not just a game? That even in a family concern, plans have to be adhered to?"

"Oh, don't be so rigid," Gene exclaimed impatiently, following him inside, while Ashleigh trailed along behind. "I wanted to get Belle home. All that row was upsetting her, so I asked David to bring Ashleigh home. He'd have been back at the camp in the morning if it was all that important. I just can't understand your way of looking at things. There's no need for you or Colin or David to sleep out at the camp when it's so close to the homestead, anyhow. It's uncivilised."

"Then that's the way I like it, Gene. Uncivilised. . . . I hope at least you have some dinner ready."

"Yes." She said it half laughingly, half angrily. "There's a roast and vegetables in the oven."

"Good. . . . I'll take a shower."

He crossed the hall and went up the stairs, and Ashleigh stood biting her lip. She'd caused a lot of trouble and she didn't quite know why, exactly. Gene had left her to be brought home by David, unless she was trying to help him along in his search for a wife. If that was the case, Gene was wasting her time pushing him in Ashleigh's direction.

"That brother of mine," Gene muttered. "I don't know why I hang around here. I wish he'd hurry up and marry, that's all." She looked at Ashleigh and grimaced. "He *is* uncivilised. Debra would soon smarten him up. She's rational and sane and strong-minded too. Just what he needs. Oh well, the boys will be home when the muster's over."

And would she still be here? Ashleigh wondered. Or would Charlie and Ryan between them have engineered things so she could be on her way to Darwin by then? She contemplated the thought with reluctance. She was far from confident about driving all that way by herself.

Ryan didn't go back to the cattle camp next day. When Ashleigh went down to breakfast, she was disconcerted to find him sitting at the table, casually dressed in jeans and open-necked shirt, his hair damp from the shower, his eyes enigmatic and somehow hard. Out on the back verandah, Gene was busy with Belle, and that meant that he and Ashleigh were alone. She sat down quickly, sent him a guarded smile, and reached for the coffee-pot.

"I thought you'd have gone back to the camp by this time," she commented.

"Did you? Now I'm home, I'll stay here. I might as well give my brothers a clear run," he said, glancing at her briefly. "There's always plenty to keep me busy, particularly when travellers break down and want assistance. . . . I rang Kununurra this morning about those spare parts, by the way. I'll see Charlie has time to work on your boyfriend's vehicle as soon as they arrive."

"Thank you," she said stiffly. "I'll pay for the telephone call of course, and for the work your mechanic puts in on the car. In his spare time," she added.

He slanted her a look. "My mechanic's not for hire, Miss Stevens. He's on my payroll."

"I know that. But surely what he does in his spare time is his own affair," she retorted.

"We don't measure spare time by city standards in the bush."

And what was that supposed to mean? she wondered angrily. Charlie must have *some* spare time when he could please himself what he did. And of course, he'd want to spend it with his wife and children, she realised instantly. She shrugged mentally. Ryan could make a martyr of himself or a scapegoat of her or whatever it was he was trying to do. Her head lowered, she went on eating her breakfast.

"I'll make sure you have an escort when the time comes," he said coldly after a moment of silence, and Ashleigh seethed inwardly and wondered why she'd

ever imagined she was even physically attracted to such
an unpredictable and disagreeable man.

"You don't have to pile it on," she said icily. "I won't
need an escort. Whatever your opinion of me is, I
assure you I can manage perfectly well on my own."
She swallowed down some of her coffee and met his
mocking eyes over her cup.

"It's not a case of my opinion of you, Ashleigh," he
said dryly. "I'm merely going by what your boyfriend
thinks, and I'm sure he knows you a whole lot better
than I do. The radio news from Darwin is that he's
comfortable, by the way. And he sent you a message,"
he added, his aquamarine eyes glinting. "Not very
personal, but to the point. 'Slow down in creek beds,
and don't take any more wrong turnings.' Which seems
to make a lot of sense, don't you think? Particularly the
latter part."

He pushed back his chair as he spoke, and Ashleigh
was quite sure there was a double meaning in what he
said. She'd taken more than one wrong turning since
she'd met Ryan Langton, and that was a fact. But
wasn't he at fault too? Like Don, it seemed he wanted
to put all the blame on her.

He stood looking down at her and she looked back at
him, in spite of the fact that she could feel the blood
rushing to her face so that it was a fiery red. She
swallowed angrily and told herself that she hated him
and that she wished she'd never met him.

"What would you like to do today?" he asked,
suddenly polite, and she snapped back not at all
politely, "You needn't worry about me. I don't want to
make myself a nuisance to anyone."

One eyebrow rose. "No?" He stretched his arms
over his head, the movement emphasising the muscles
of his chest, the narrowness of his hips. "Well, whether
you like it or not, you are a nuisance, Ashleigh Stevens.

A damned nuisance." He sent her an enigmatic look, then turned on his heel and was gone.

"Thanks," Ashleigh muttered, her cheeks still burning. She returned to her breakfast frowningly. That man . . . he upset her, he confused her. She'd be glad when the car was fixed and she could return to her own life. It was a great pity he hadn't stayed out at the cattle camp and let David bring her back to the homestead. As long as he was around there was turmoil. There was nothing surer.

But the turmoil had to wait, because whatever he was doing, she saw nothing more of him that day.

Ashleigh spent the day innocuously, soporifically, almost boringly about the homestead with Gene and Belle. The highlight of the day, in fact, was watching Selma Gray making bread in the homestead kitchen— some for her own family, some for the Langtons. Ashleigh had never made bread, and she found the process fascinating. If I lived here, she caught herself thinking, I'd bake my own bread.

But of course she'd never live here. . . .

She was quite resigned by now to waiting some days for the car to be fixed. But why shouldn't she tow it back to the homestead herself, with Gene's cooperation? It would be one way of showing Ryan that she wasn't content to sit back and let everything be done for her.

But when she suggested it, Gene rejected the idea at once. "We don't have to kill ourselves trailing out there and hitching the car up and towing it all the way home. Charlie will do that. It's all in the day's work for him."

Ashleigh felt frustrated, but there was nothing to be done about it. Obviously, Gene preferred to spend the day in the garden or reading on the verandah, or playing with Belle.

In the afternoon, eager for some kind of action,

Ashleigh wandered away beyond the homestead gardens, to take a look at the numerous bungalows and buildings that made up a complex almost the size of a small village. There was even a little schoolhouse where the aboriginal children had lessons. There were horses too, and she'd have liked to go for a ride, but that would entail getting permission from Ryan, she supposed, and reluctantly let it go.

He appeared at dinner time, looking as if he'd just showered, and wearing light pants and a black, collarless shirt that gave him a rather devilish look. The meal was a rather silent one. Gene complained of a headache and responded unenthusiastically when Ryan gave her the news that Debra Davis would be arriving in a few days' time, bringing another girl with her.

"About the right age for David, I gather," he added. He sent Ashleigh a swift glance before continuing, "What did you girls do today?"

"Ashleigh got enthusiastic about bread-making," Gene said. "And we watered the garden and romped on the lawn with Belle and Josh. Oh, and Ashleigh took a walk. She had a riotous day, in fact."

His eyes narrowed and went to Ashleigh. She could practically hear him thinking, I told you it wouldn't be all pleasure. "You were bored, I suppose. I half-expected to hear you'd shot off to the cattle camp again."

"Did you?" She gave him a cool look, which suddenly turned to something else, so that she had to avert her eyes. Damn! Why did he have to do this to her?

When the meal was over, Ashleigh helped Gene stack the dishes and then found herself left alone in the sitting room to watch TV, because Gene's headache was bad and she'd gone up to bed. Ryan, presumably, was in the office again, avoiding her. Well, she certainly didn't want to spend the evening with him, she told herself. She thought about Don, wondered how he was, and tried to calculate how long it would be before she got to Darwin. What would happen then? she wondered. Their plans—hers and Don's—had been turned topsy turvy; but, like Debra, he was a strong character, and he'd work something out. At least she would be able to take over from Caryl once she'd learned the ropes, even though Don wouldn't be able to do the driving.

The thought didn't excite her as it once would have done. Somehow it all seemed unreal, even futile. And Laura, she thought suddenly. She'd scarcely given a thought to Laura in days. It was a little cheering to think that most likely she'd be in Darwin too by the time she got there.

Switching off the television, she wandered onto the verandah. The night air was full of the sweet scents of the garden, and she leaned against the rail trying to analyse them, kicking off her sandals and feeling the coolness of the stone floor under her feet. The sky was bright with stars, and she sought out the Southern Cross, at the dipping end of the Milky Way. How lovely it was here, she thought. The peaceful sounds of the night, the sense of wonder invoked by the immensity of it all. Yes, this was where she belonged. . . .

Well, not exactly *here*, she amended the thought quickly. But in this part of the world. Not back in Perth amongst city people who rarely took time off to meditate and let the things that mattered sink in. It was hard to understand why someone like Gene, who had been born here, should long to go back to the city.

Somebody came onto the verandah and she swung round to find it was Ryan.

"Oh—I thought you were doing your paperwork," she exclaimed unevenly, feeling her heart begin to race.

"I've finished up for the night. . . . Where's Gene?"

"She went to bed with a headache. I was watching TV but—there's more to see out here," she finished with an uncertain smile.

"Ah, the night, the stars. Yes, it's very romantic, isn't it?" He'd come to stand close to her and her body started its familiar and maddening response to his nearness.

She moved a little away from him. "I—I think I'll go in to bed now."

He said nothing, and she didn't go. She looked up at him through her lashes and was disconcerted to find he was looking back at her, his eyes darkly mysterious, the line of his mouth curving slightly.

They stared at each other for a long moment, neither of them moving, neither of them speaking. Ashleigh knew what she wanted and despised herself for it, and she moistened her lips nervously.

"Well," he said at last, his eyes still on hers, "I thought you said you were going in to bed. What's keeping you?"

She swallowed painfully. "Nothing. . . . Good night." She turned away jerkily and immediately he reached out to grasp her wrist and pull her back.

"Were you waiting for a good night kiss, Ashleigh Stevens? Is that it?" he asked, his voice so savage that she shivered.

"No, that's not it," she exclaimed fiercely, knowing in her heart that it was. "I was here first. I wasn't waiting for you."

"No, but I came, didn't I?" His fingers were tight around her wrist and she could feel her blood racing. "And after all, it's my verandah," he added with a wry smile.

She wrested her arm out of his grip.

"You hate me being here, don't you? Well, believe me, I don't want to stay any longer than I have to. And I—I wish you'd leave me alone."

She turned and fled inside, through the softly lit sitting room and up the stairs to her bedroom, where she locked the door and stood looking across at her mirrored reflection. Her face was flushed, her eyes bright, and somewhere inside she was close to tears—of anger, of a curious hurt. She didn't know what to make of Ryan Langton, or of herself either. All she knew for certain was that they were physically attracted to each other, and that for her, at least, it was dangerous. . . .

She had what she'd asked for over the next couple of days. Ryan left her alone. He disappeared straight after breakfast. She didn't know where he went, and she didn't ask. She tried her hand at bread-making while Gene supervised the house-girls, they went for walks with the children, and Ashleigh took an interest in the garden. She had no more encounters with Ryan after dinner. She made sure of that, though undoubtedly she had his full cooperation.

So she almost fell over with surprise when one morning he suggested very pleasantly and civilly that they should all go for a picnic and a swim to the Crystal Pool. Ashleigh's heart lightened, in spite of herself. She was a little tired of the inactive life at the homestead, and she eagerly helped Gene prepare a picnic lunch.

Belle collected Josh and they set off in the Land Rover, Gene with the children in the back, Ashleigh sitting beside Ryan in the front seat, but keeping well away from him.

It was a long drive: over the open grasslands where Mitchell and Flinders grass waved, then into rugged country and red rocky hills covered with cushiony spinifex and white-trunked snappy gums that Ryan called black hearts. She was entranced when at last they entered the gorge where the pool lay. It was like an enchanted place, boabs and wattles and paper-barks making purple shadows on the red ground, small yellow-and-blue flowers growing in clusters, all of it brooded over by sheer orange-red cliffs that looked like the ruins of an ancient fort.

The Crystal Pool lay at the base of one of these cliffs, on whose glistening surface green plants—small flowering shrubs and lush leafed vines—grew in profusion.

"You'd see a waterfall there in the Wet," Ryan commented. "But as the Dry progresses, the rock face gradually dries out and the plants die. The pool stays. Pretty, isn't it?"

She nodded. It was more than pretty, it was beautiful —the water pale green like chrysoprase, and so clear you could see right down to the clean river sand and the waterworn boulders underneath. Dragon-flies skimmed about above a patch of white and blue water-lilies, and the air was warm and still. Ashleigh drew a deep breath. People said this was a harsh land, but she was learning that there was beauty hidden in it, particularly in the deep gorges cut into the ancient sandstones by rivers that raged in the Wet and diminished into strings of waterholes in the Dry. She had a growing feeling of being in tune with it, but that was something she couldn't tell Ryan, who was sure to find it suspect.

They ate their picnic lunch sitting on a rug spread out in the shade of the giant kajeputs that leaned over the water. Then, while Ashleigh and Gene tidied everything away, Ryan took the two small children for a walk.

"Why don't you go too, Ashleigh?" Gene suggested. She'd produced a book from the Land Rover and was preparing to stretch out on the rug in the shade. "I'm going to have a read till the kids come back. Then I'll have to keep an eye on them while they play in the water."

Ashleigh hesitated. If she ran after Ryan now, it would quite likely invite some scathing comment such as the one he'd handed out to her the other night. She decided to take the opposite direction and sauntered slowly along through the trees. The hakeas were bright with big bunches of red flowers, and the silver-leafed grevilleas were coming into bloom. Wattles, heavy with masses of fluffy golden blossoms, scented the air muskily, and there were paper-barks by the score. Ashleigh paused to peel some of the pale pink and grey bark away from the limb of an ancient tree. It was so soft and velvety to touch that it was easy to understand why the aboriginal women used it to line the coolamons in which they carried their babies.

On the edge of the pool, she stopped walking and stood gazing half-hypnotised at the crystal clear water running gently over the smooth stones. Red and blue dragon-flies skimmed silently about, and she started when a small bird flashed down from a tree to seize one, then rose almost vertically to its look-out post again. A few yards away, three grey birds with tall pointed crests came dancing daintily down to the water, flicking up their tails as if to show they were not afraid of her.

"Those are spinifex pigeons, if you're wondering," Ryan's voice said and she looked round to find him standing only a few feet away. His blue glance made her heart-beats quicken, and she smiled briefly, then looked back at the pigeons.

"Saucy, aren't they?" he commented. "They often land away from the water and walk to it to drink. . . . That other bird a minute ago was a rainbow bird. And over there—between those two rocks—that's a bower-bird flapping about. He has a playground somewhere around. We might take a look, if you like. Or are you ready for a swim?"

"Not yet. I'd rather look for the bower-bird's playground," she said, a little warily, enjoying his company in his present mellow mood.

He found the bower in an amazingly short space of

time, then admitted with a smile that he'd visited it before. It was under a wattle tree and Ashleigh stooped to look at it curiously. It was a walk-through bower made of sticks woven together to form an archway about a foot high. At each side was a collection of bleached bones, shells, quartz crystals, and bits of glass, mostly white, but with a scattering of green.

"The objects right inside the bower are the ornaments he particularly favours," Ryan said, stooping too. "I suppose you know it's not a nest but a place for courting. Once a female's attracted, the male bird puts on a display and woos her. They mate, she builds her nest, and he stays with his playground. And if there's a parallel to be drawn somewhere then I don't want to know about it," he added with a laugh that showed the whiteness of his teeth. "If we come back a little later, we might find him here singing or rearranging his treasures. . . . Meanwhile shall we have that swim?"

They walked back companionably to where Gene was watching the children, now in their swimsuits, playing on the edge of the water, building castles and digging moats in the coarse sand.

Ashleigh, who by now was feeling surprisingly at ease with Ryan, fished out her bikini from the Land Rover and disappeared into the trees to change, then emerged a little self-consciously in the two tiny scraps of sugary cinnamon and pink fabric. Ryan was already in the water, swimming lazily along at the far side beneath the shadow of the cliff, where it must be deeper, Ashleigh surmised. She waded in, walking until the water deepened, and then she swam too. The water was soft and not at all cold, and she swam and floated for some time, gradually drifting along with the slow, gentle current.

The car and the children and Gene were all out of sight when she saw Ryan swim towards the bank, reach shallow water, and stand up, raking his fingers through his wet hair before making his way over half-submerged rocks onto the sand.

Ashleigh followed him. He turned to watch her as she came towards him, moving carefully over the flat stones that gleamed palely through the glassy water.

Right at the last minute, she slipped and grabbed wildly at him, laughing as she regained her balance, her arms around his waist.

Then as she met his eyes her laughter died. Suddenly she was aware of the feel of his naked flesh under her hands. She lifted her face and the next moment she was crushed against him and her passion rose in a wave as he kissed her hard, their mouths still wet from the water, their bodies clinging. One of his hands moved exploringly down her back to rest at the base of her spine, the other slid up from her waist to the curve of her breast, only just decently covered by the tiny bikini bra.

And then—she didn't know how it happened—he'd lifted her into his arms and carried her under the trees, and she didn't even think of protesting when he lay down with her on the clean, coarse sand and began kissing her again.

Soon their legs were twined together and her arms were around him and she was kissing him back as though she couldn't help herself. It was the sexiest embrace she could ever have imagined, and she was half frightened, half excited at the pressure of his bare thighs against her own. She knew exactly and explicitly what they wanted of each other and she was shocked at herself. She'd never thought of herself as a sensual or passionate girl, but right now all her inhibitions were being swept away by the strength of her desire for Ryan Langton.

The sun burned down on them through the leaning branches of the paper-barks, vaguely she could hear the screeching of the black cockatoos, but even that seemed no more than an extension of her feeling for him. She was hardly aware of his kisses any more, because kissing was merely a part of the whole. Their bodies, perilously close to naked, were locked together, and she had parted her lips to let his tongue explore her mouth while she answered with a strange kind of effortlessness the demands his body made on her.

When at last his mouth left hers, she gave a gasp and let her head fall back on the sand. He leaned over her and they stared silently into each other's eyes. Ashleigh lay so still it was as if she couldn't move. She could feel his body heavy and cool, yet warm and pulsing with life, on her own and she could see the dark spikes of his lashes, the black dilated pupils of his eyes, with the blue-and-green flowers of his irises radiating out from them. She felt she was seeing right into the centre of his being. It was as if she were discovering another human being in a way that had never happened to her before.

That slow, intent, silent exploration of each other's eyes was like a revelation, because she knew he was discovering her in the same way. It wasn't physical—it wasn't just about sex, though it was that too. It went deeper than that, into the mystery of being male and female, of love and understanding.

He didn't kiss her again. After what seemed an eternity, he moved away from her slowly, sitting back on his heels and looking down at her where she lay. His blue eyes followed the lines of her body from her throat across her breast to her waist, her stomach, her thighs, while she lay there feeling not in the least self-conscious, feeling nothing but a kind of intense and concentrated pleasure. When he got up and reached out a hand to her, she took it and let him pull her to her feet and lead her back through the trees in the direction of the car and the sounds of the children as they shouted and laughed at their play.

They exchanged a slow smile as they emerged from

the paper-barks; then he dropped her hand and said casually, "Better get dressed."

They parted. Feeling almost dazed, she collected her pants and top and disappeared to dress. Gene had spoken to her and she thought she'd answered, but she didn't really know what either of them had said.

The rest of the day was a blur. Ryan, with the children's help, built a small fire and they boiled the billy and made tea, ate the cakes and scones they'd brought with them, and then, when everything was packed up again, they piled into the car and set off for the homestead. Ashleigh sat beside Ryan again. A couple of times their thighs touched and more than a couple of times she glanced at him through her lashes. But he didn't talk and he didn't look at her, not until they were back at the homestead, when he asked her, his voice curiously clipped, "Enjoy yourself?"

"Very much," she said huskily, and he smiled crook-edly.

# Chapter Seven

That night Ashleigh lay in bed in the dark thinking of what had happened out at the Crystal Pool. Thinking of the way she and Ryan had looked into each other's eyes. It had been like a glimpse of something tantalisingly desirable yet out of reach—more stirring, more important, than any kisses they had exchanged. More pleasurable. She tried to relive the experience, but it was impossible. She'd been intoxicated by what she'd felt, but now when she tried to call it back, the exquisite pleasure of it eluded her. It had been like a taste of paradise, of Eden, and it had all seemed so right and so wonderful. She wanted desperately to see him again—to look in his eyes—to find out what it all meant.

At dinner, they'd exchanged glances during a conversation that had been mainly about the bird life on Crystal Downs. But there had been nothing personal or intimate, and she'd been disappointed when afterwards he sat in the sitting room and read for a short while and then with a muttered excuse disappeared.

"He's got the muster on the brain," Gene had said with a yawn. "The boys will have got the cattle to the loading yards by now, ready for the road train to pick them up tomorrow. And then they'll all be home."

"How do you know?" Ashleigh had asked.

"Ryan said so. He keeps his finger on the pulse—with the aid of two-way radio," Gene added with a laugh. "I'm willing to bet he'll be off at daylight to do some supervising. Well, it will be nice to have a bit of social life, won't it? And in a couple of days Debra and her friend will be here as well."

Thinking of that as she lay in bed, Ashleigh felt her stomach churn. It was clear that Debra was the girl Gene believed Ryan was going to marry. The thought of Debra's being here was almost too painful to be borne. Slightly panic-stricken, Ashleigh tried to think of Don, but it didn't seem to help. On the contrary, in fact.

She closed her eyes and tried an old childish trick of reciting poetry: *"Ah rose, thou art sick—"*

A soft knocking on the door made her sit up, startled, and her eyes, accustomed to the darkness, saw the door open and the dark shadow of a man come into the room. His bare torso gleamed above white pants, and she gasped silently. It was Ryan. She stared at him, unable to speak as he moved towards her.

"Ashleigh? Are you awake?" She could feel him looking at her and she heard the bed creak softly as he sat down on the side of it.

"I guess you can't sleep. . . . Don't feel too guilty about this afternoon. Nothing happened," he said, his voice low.

She listened, her heart thudding. Was that what he'd come to say to her? She couldn't believe it—she knew it wasn't what she'd expected deep down inside of her.

And how could he possibly say that nothing had happened? It just wasn't true, and surely he knew it. *Everything* had happened—it had been world-shattering. But of course that was only the way she saw it.

"Did you hear what I said, Ashleigh?"

She nodded, her throat dry. "Yes—I heard," she said miserably. She wondered if he was talking this way because Debra would soon be here, and he had to make sure she didn't get any wrong ideas about her importance to him.

She lay back on the pillow and flung her arm across her face.

"Don't worry. I've just about forgotten it. I really don't know what you're going on about. It . . . it surely wasn't all that important."

"No," he said after a moment and then told her almost savagely, "don't think I'm proud of myself, making love to you the way I did. I wish to God it had never happened. But you asked for it, and you know it."

"You mean it was all my fault," she said bitterly. She was close to tears, hurt, angry.

"Not entirely." He got up from the bed. "However, let's say no more about it."

Ashleigh didn't answer him. Nor did she respond to his brief "Good night," as he went silently across the room and disappeared.

Tears had gathered in her eyes and she let them fall, feeling them run down the side of her face into her hair and onto the pillow. Forget it? How could she? She'd said it wasn't all that important, but it was. Of course it was. Until he'd come and shattered her dreams just now, it had seemed the most important thing that had ever happened in the whole of her life. And in her heart, she knew why. Because she'd fallen in love with him—hopelessly.

She turned on her face and stifled the sob that had risen in her throat. If only that replacement part would come; if only Charlie would perform some miracle and get Don's car on the road so she could disappear from here. She couldn't stand much more of this kind of torture.

She slept at last from sheer exhaustion, her pillow wet with futile tears.

In the morning, it seemed as if her miracle might happen. When she looked down from the window of her room, there was Don's car standing on the drive. Charlie had towed it back to the homestead, and rescue was at hand.

She dressed hurriedly, not bothering to use any make-up, and ran down the stairs and through to kitchen. Gene was there with Belle, but there was no sign of Ryan.

"Where's Charlie?" she demanded, and Gene stared at her as if she'd gone out of her mind.

"He left an hour ago for Kununurra."

Ashleigh's eyes widened. "You mean he's gone to get the—the sump or tray or whatever it is for Don's car?"

Gene shook her head. "He has to catch the plane to Port Hedland. His father's had a stroke and isn't expected to live. His mother needs him there."

Ashleigh came down to earth with a thud. She sat down at the table and reached for the coffee pot. "Oh . . . I'm sorry. I had no idea. I just thought—"

Her voice trailed off and Gene said wryly, "You really do want to get away, don't you? I was hoping you were enjoying yourself here. But don't worry. You'll get to Darwin long before Don Harris is able to drive a car again. And it might cheer you up to know I heard Ryan tell Charlie to pick up the spare parts on his way back."

Ashleigh managed a smile. It looked as though her departure was further off than ever, which meant she'd

have to steel herself to endure more agony from her
encounters with Ryan. If only things were different, she
thought hopelessly.

"Anyhow," Gene said, "the boys will be back tonight. You'll have a much better time when they're
around."

Perhaps she would, Ashleigh thought. At least having a few more people about the place would help to
keep her mind off Ryan.

The mail came that day, and Ashleigh drove out with
Gene and Belle to the landing strip to collect it. No
spare parts, of course. Charlie was to bring them when
he picked up his car in Kununurra, and goodness knows
when that would be.

"Expecting any letters?" Gene asked as they drove
back to the homestead, the mail-bag and various goods
that had been ordered stowed away in the back of the
car.

"Not really," Ashleigh said. "Except from Don,"
she added, wondering if he might have written.

"I'm afraid you'll have to wait till Ryan comes home
to find out. I wouldn't dare open the mail-bag," Gene
apologised. "Though if you're really anxious—"

"I can wait," Ashleigh shrugged. She didn't want to
cause trouble by inciting Gene to break the station
rules.

In spite of everything, she found it exciting when the
boys arrived home that night, after seeing the cattle
loaded onto the road trains: David, Colin, and Ryan
too. It was just before dark and the sky was a smoky
red when they heard the cars coming up the drive.
Gene ran out onto the verandah and Ashleigh, who had
been in the kitchen helping her prepare a dinner that
seemed enormous, went out too.

The car lamps, muted in the twilight, swung in a wide
circle as the cars came round the drive towards the
house. One car horn tooted.

"That's Colin, the mad fool," Gene exclaimed laughing.

The other followed suit; then, with a screeching of brakes, both cars pulled up in front of the homestead. The doors flew open and the men emerged.

Ashleigh stood on the verandah shivering with excitement, almost as if she were part of this family and this was part of her life. Belle had come down from upstairs in her natty little pink pyjamas just as if she knew all about it, and even Gene, who professed to hate the outback, was laughing with delight. She raced down the steps and after a second Ashleigh followed her. Colin grabbed his sister around the waist and waltzed away with her along the drive, and before Ashleigh knew what was happening, David had seized hold of her, kissed her fervently, shouted "Halloo!" and whirled her around until she was dizzy.

They were all laughing as they went up the steps onto the verandah. Ashleigh had given Ryan only one quick look. He had Belle in his arms and he looked back at her over the child's dark head and smiled in a tight-lipped way that made it clear *he* didn't regard her as part of the family. Somehow she couldn't help remembering what he'd said about fascinating David. Biting her lip, she headed for the kitchen, away from the others. She felt trapped, enmeshed in her own emotions, knowing how much she wanted Ryan to be . . . just to be nice to her, that was all.

Presently, Gene came to join her in the kitchen and the men went upstairs to make themselves presentable for dinner.

Talk was non-stop at the dinner table, and over and over again Ashleigh found David's eyes on her. But not Ryan's. He was cool, aloof, and very polite, and it was partly because of that that she played up to David, smiling at him, directing her attention and her questions to him, agreeing eagerly when he invited her to go riding with him in the morning.

When they went through to the verandah with their coffee afterwards, Ryan excused himself and went to the office to deal with the mail.

It was some time before he came back. By then, the boys were playing taped music. They'd all been fooling about, dancing on the stone flagged floor, and Ashleigh was beginning to see what Ryan had meant when he'd said she'd have no trouble fascinating his brother. David showed every sign of being all set to fall in love with her, and that was something she'd have to watch.

She was standing by herself, her back against the verandah rail, when she saw Ryan come to the door and her heart gave a thump. David had gone to hunt out a particular cassette he wanted Ashleigh to hear and Colin and Gene were busy pouring themselves glasses of soft drink.

Ryan came straight across to Ashleigh.

"Some mail for you, Ashleigh." He handed her a letter, then dropped his voice so that only she could hear. "Go easy on my brother, will you? Just don't start anything you're not prepared to finish." His startlingly blue eyes looked at her intently and she dropped her lashes. Suddenly her body was burning as she remembered the kisses, the long exploring looks they'd exchanged only yesterday under the paper-barks by the pool. Her mind had drifted right away from what he was saying and she jumped when he asked savagely, "Do I make myself clear?"

"Perfectly," she stammered, her blood turning to ice. "But why save all your warnings or threats or whatever for me? I'm not the one who's making the running."

He smiled cynically. "Who do you think you're fooling? I know too much about you to believe that. . . . But if you want to play dumb—if that sort of thing turns you on—then crash around and break all the hearts you can in the time that's available to you." His eyes had darkened, and he swung away from her as David came back. "I've just delivered some fan mail to Ashleigh," he said shortly. "I suggest you leave her in peace while she reads it."

David raised his eyebrows and sent Ashleigh a puzzled look.

"What's that all about?" he demanded as Ryan strode away. He glanced down at the letter she was holding and she noticed her hand was trembling. "Do you want to read your letter? Or are we going to dance?"

"My letter can wait," she said with a swift, defiant look in Ryan's direction, which he didn't even see. "Let's dance."

Idiotically, she wished as David put his arms around her that Ryan would break in, dance with her himself, hold her closely, crush her against his body. . . . They were painful thoughts that provoked painful emotions, especially as Ryan didn't even look at her. He'd joined the others, handed Gene some letters, and poured himself a drink. Ashleigh watched him over David's shoulder and though he seemed unaware of her, she knew he wasn't.

"I've been invited to a wedding in Perth," Gene exclaimed a moment later.

"You'll go?" Ryan asked and she said she would.

"You'll just have to find someone else to look after you while I'm away—persuade Debra to stay on—or Ashleigh."

"I'll persuade you to stay, Ashleigh," David whispered, and Ashleigh looked at him exasperatedly. She'd have to watch out or she'd be having problems with David.

A moment later, still without a glance for her, Ryan went inside, and she felt her spirits slump. She danced with David a little longer. Then she excused herself and went upstairs, after assuring him that she'd be ready for a ride right after breakfast in the morning and privately determining that she'd persuade him somehow to cool off her—not because of anything Ryan had said, but because she knew it wasn't fair. She was never likely to fall the least little bit in love with him. Her emotions were engaged fully and futilely elsewhere.

In her room, she switched on the lamp, lay down on the bed, and read Don's letter. It was the first time he'd ever written to her, and his handwriting was quite unfamiliar. So was his style, and though it was fluent, it didn't give her the thrill it would have if she'd still been wild about him the way she was before they left Perth. Don, she realised with a sharp little feeling of disbelief, had in a way been her hero in those days. He wasn't anymore, and it wasn't solely because she knew him better.

It seemed he'd been kept up to date with what was happening about the car and in fact knew more than she did about what repairs would be necessary: an engine overhaul, probably new rings and bearings as well as a new sump. He didn't know that Charlie had gone to Port Hedland, and naturally Don took it for granted that after mail-day everything would go ahead rapidly.

I guess you have the money to pay for all this. I'll settle up with you when you come to Darwin. I'll be out of the hospital in four or five days and I'll go straight to the Carsons. Hope you'll like the house, because I'm buying it. I know you'll like Len and Caryl. They're going to let you get stuck into the hostessing straight away so you can take over from Caryl. Len will carry on until I'm fit to drive. I've been told my knee will be as good as ever, so don't worry about that. In the meantime,

I'll get myself really clued up on the flora, fauna, geology, history et cetera, of the Top End.

He went on to say that he'd heard from Laura, who, predictably, he said, was chickening out. She had been sick, but was now over the worst of it. Instead of coming on to Darwin, Laura would be returning to Perth.

I'll write and let her know the news from our end. Take care with the car, won't you? Darwin's a long way, but I know you can do it.

That, Ashleigh reflected thoughtfully, was a distinct about-face. He'd said before that she had no road sense, and he hadn't said it politely. But perhaps that had been in the heat of the moment. . . .

He signed himself, *"Lovingly, Don."*

It wasn't the sort of letter to make any girl's heart beat faster, but she supposed it was a reflection of his personality. Practical, down to earth, and definitely not romantic. One thing that did come across was that he expected her to share his future.

She let the letter fall to the floor and put her hands behind her head and stared at the ceiling. What was she going to do about Don? She couldn't let him simply take it for granted that she was his for the asking. And yet he hadn't really given her a chance to tell him one way or the other if she'd marry him. It would have to wait until she got to Darwin; that was all.

She went riding with David next day, wearing the most practical clothes she could root out: pale lemon jeans and a long-sleeved white-and-yellow shirt. Ryan's eyes flicked over her enigmatically when she came downstairs.

"Can you ride, Ashleigh?" he asked in a soft voice as she passed him on her way to the verandah.

"Barely," she said icily and added on impulse, "I might have to ask David to hold me on."

His blue eyes blazed, but he said no more.

As it happened, she was quite a capable rider, having learned at school. For a while she'd even belonged to a pony club, until she'd had a fall. After that, her subscription was cancelled. "We're responsible for your safety, Ashleigh," Esme had said adamantly.

She enjoyed her ride with David, though she found it an exercise in ingenuity to avoid a romantic interlude under the trees by the waterhole. He was intent on engineering it, and she was equally intent on avoiding it, and somehow she managed to win, partly by talking about Darwin and her plans for the future.

"Unfortunately, Don won't be able to do any driving for awhile, and that means we have to think one or two things through again," she said casually. "But he said in his letter he's confident everything will work out all right for us eventually."

"For us?" David repeated, looking crestfallen. "Exactly what do you mean by that?" He was riding alongside her and, seeing the expression on his face, she felt really mean. "Are you by any chance planning to marry this bloke, Ashleigh?"

"That was the idea when I left Perth," she said flushing a little.

There was a short silence and then David said persuasively, "I could make you change your mind if you stayed around Crystal Downs a bit longer."

She bit her lip. "I don't think you'd better try, David."

"No?" His eyebrows went up and he gave her a wicked smile. "How are you going to stop me?"

Ashleigh touched her horse's flank with her heel and raced ahead of him and he followed, shouting laughingly that you couldn't keep a good man down.

That afternoon they played tennis on the hard red

antbed tennis court. Gene wasn't playing, the sun was hot, and after a couple of strenuous sets, Ashleigh decided she needed a break. If she'd thought the men would play cutthroat or toss for singles, she was wrong. Ryan left the court to his two brothers and came to join her in the shade of the trees where she was sitting.

"You don't have to make a martyr of yourself and keep me company," she said unsmilingly, though she'd had no intention of saying any such thing.

He looked at her through narrowed eyes. "You know damned well I'm far from averse to your company, Ashleigh."

"Do I?" She nearly added, "You seem to have been getting along very well without it lately." Instead, she twisted her tennis racquet in her hands and asked him pointedly, "When are Debra and her friend coming?"

"Around midday tomorrow," he said. "Are you looking forward to it?"

"Yes, of course," she said brightly. "But I won't be here to enjoy their company for very long."

"It might be for longer than you think," he said dryly. "Charlie won't be back for several days. The news of his father isn't good. However, I'm sure you'll be able to put in the time flirting with someone. You seem to have quite a bit of expertise in that direction."

She flushed angrily. "What's that supposed to mean?"

"First me, now David," he said with a crooked smile. "You were putting on a very pretty show on the court a few minutes ago. And you certainly got away to a good start this morning. What does it feel like to have men falling at your feet like ninepins?"

"I wouldn't know," she said, hurt. She got to her feet. "I'm going inside," she said briefly, and went.

After dinner that night, David invited her to go for a walk with him in the garden, and she refused point blank.

David looked at her consideringly, his handsome face serious for once. "You mean you're really in love with that bloke who owns the car? Just my luck. . . . Oh well, there's still this stunning little American girl who's arriving with Debra tomorrow—standing on tippy toes with eagerness to meet the one and only heart-whole Langton lad," he added with a return to his usual bantering manner. "When you see another girl rush into my arms, you might well decide to try and get there first, Ashleigh darling. We shall see."

Ashleigh laughed, relieved that he took such a light-hearted view of it all.

The American girl, Betty-Lou Burhans, *was* stunning, in a natural friendly way, and Ashleigh liked her at once. She was out from Georgia on a visit to her uncle who ran cattle in the Top End. She'd met Debra when she was staying in Darwin for a week with her aunt, an Australian, and she confessed candidly that she'd heard all about "you Langton guys," and that she was thrilled to have been invited to stay at Crystal Downs. She and Debra arrived in time for lunch, as predicted, and Ashleigh learned very quickly that Debra knew all about her being there, and all about Don's accident.

"There's a great big welcome waiting for you at Caryl Carson's," she remarked over lunch, which they were having al fresco, in the shade of the Indian rain trees. "She tells me you and Don are buying their house. You'll love it. It's built on stilts in the old style, but reinforced against cyclones, of course," she finished with a smile.

Everyone was listening, and Ashleigh was fully aware that Debra's insinuation that she and Don were going to be married had come across loud and clear. She felt Ryan's eyes on her, but didn't dare meet them, and she was also aware that David's attention was switched very rapidly to Betty-Lou. As of that moment, he abandoned his pursuit of her in favour of the American girl. She was a pretty girl of about Ashleigh's own age, with curly blonde hair, a tip-tilted nose, freckles, and an engagingly candid air, and she didn't seem to be at all averse to having David flirt with her.

That was fine as far as Ashleigh was concerned. She could do without the complication of having David pursue her. As for Ryan, did it matter what he thought? Now that Debra was here, she should be thankful to have him believe her affections were engaged elsewhere. It would save her pride, if nothing else.

As Colin had predicted, things livened up in the following days. The hours were filled with riding, tennis, picnics, and barbecues, a lot of talk and plenty of laughter. David spent every minute possible with Betty-Lou. They talked together endlessly and animatedly, and he showed her everything there was to be seen around the station. And Ryan, as Ashleigh had known he would, devoted himself to Debra, taking her out to the calf branding with him or wherever he happened to be going. Ashleigh stayed around the homestead with Gene. The Langton men, she reflected, certainly didn't let their hearts rule their heads. Nor did they let the grass grow under their feet, judging by David's performance.

She didn't care what David did, but it was agony to see Debra and Ryan constantly together. Ashleigh had had no idea it would hurt so much, and she struggled with herself in an attempt to accept the situation. She'd been taught that intelligence consists in changing what can be changed, and accepting what can't, and while David had obviously done exactly that, she found that for her it was far from easy. She forced herself to concentrate on Don, to whom they all thought she was engaged, anyhow. Who knew, she might even discover that she was madly in love with him, when she met him again! Ryan had heard from Charlie that his father had died, and that after the funeral he'd stay on a few days to settle things before coming back to Crystal Downs, so it wasn't going to be all that long.

Meanwhile, acutely aware of the fact that by rights she shouldn't be part of this house party at all, Ashleigh did what she could to help Gene, particularly with the cooking. That gave her a lot of satisfaction, and there were other times too when she managed to forget her heartache and enjoy herself. Especially in the evenings when Colin brought his guitar onto the verandah and they all sang sentimental old songs like "Tennessee Waltz" and "Rose of San Antone," and sometimes Australian ballads—"Rope and Saddle Blues," "Cattle Camp Reverie"—songs that intrigued Betty-Lou, who proved to be a terrific singer. The music, the voices, the outback night—they all hit a spot right on Ashleigh's heart, and she knew that if Ryan had been in love with her it would have been heavenly.

But he wasn't in love with her. And once, when she looked up and met his eyes, he broke the contact immediately and deliberately by turning to murmur something to Debra, who was sharing the cane lounge with him, and sitting just as close to him as she could manage.

One night after dinner, Don telephoned. David answered the phone, then came into the garden where they were all talking idly and enjoying the cool night air to tell Ashleigh, "It's your boyfriend. Ropeable because you're not in Darwin, I guess." He gave her a friendly grin which told her plainly that he wasn't wasting any regrets on her now that Betty-Lou had come into his life.

"Leigh?" Don's voice was sharp. "What's happening at your end? I thought you'd have been in Darwin by this. Hasn't the car been fixed yet?"

The sound of his voice recalled him to her vividly: his

reddish beard and hair; his tall, straight figure; his hazel eyes. But it didn't thrill her in the least, and she sighed a little as she answered him. "I'm afraid nothing's been done yet, Don. Charlie had to go to Port Hedland, you see."

"Charlie? Who the heck's Charlie?" he broke in, and she told him patiently, "The mechanic. . . . His father died and I'll just have to hang around till he comes back."

"Damn and blast!" Don exploded. "I was counting on your turning up any day now. I'm staying with Len and Caryl and there's a bed ready and waiting for you. How long is it likely to be before you get here?"

"I don't know," she said, biting her lip and wishing she were as impatient about it all as he was. Heaven knew, she wasn't riotously happy where she was. "It depends when Charlie gets back," she said. "I'll keep in touch and let you know."

There was a short pause, and then he asked, "How are things progressing between Debra and Ryan?"

"What do you mean?" Ashleigh said, although she knew perfectly well.

"Well . . . are they engaged or aren't they?"

"Nothing's been said about it—yet," she said unwillingly.

"No?" Don's voice sounded strange. "Then listen, Leigh, I think you'd better come back with Debra and to hell with the car. We can arrange something about that later. I want you here. You know how I feel about you, don't you?"

Ashleigh felt her heart literally sink. She didn't want him to say he was in love with her. It was too late, and it was no use trying to tell herself otherwise.

"I'm not good at expressing my feelings," Don continued awkwardly, when she said nothing, "but I chew my nails right down when I think of you there with all those unattached blokes. Caryl says Debra only has a week's holiday, so promise me you'll ask her to give you a lift."

"All right," Ashleigh said reluctantly.

"Good." Don said something about the safari tours that she didn't take in, and then they said good bye and hung up.

She stood where she was for a long minute. She felt unhappy and horribly guilty. She should have told Don it was no use hoping anything of her, beyond having her help out with the hostessing for awhile. She could have put it tactfully, said she didn't think she'd be able to stand the climate when the Wet came—anything at all. Yet she hadn't. Well, okay, she thought wearily, she'd leave with Debra and get things sorted out with Don somehow. There was nothing to keep her here now Don didn't want her to wait for the car, and it was a pity he'd ever insisted she should. She was going to look pretty silly telling Ryan. He'd probably think he'd frozen her out. . . .

When she went back into the garden, she didn't say anything to Debra. She'd wait, she decided, and knew she was a coward. But after all, there were still two or three days left.

# Chapter Eight

The next day there was a border muster. That was to say, a neighbouring station was mustering the part of its run that bordered on Crystal Downs, and this meant there had to be someone from Crystal Downs present. David and Betty-Lou left with Colin early in the morning, and later on Ryan decided to join them. Debra went along as a matter of course, and though Ryan invited Gene and Ashleigh to join them, Gene refused point blank. Dust and heat and flies, plus crazy animals and wild stockmen racing around were not for her, she said. Ashleigh longed to go, but rather than make an unwelcome third, she refused as well, and Ryan made no effort to persuade her to change her mind.

It wasn't a day she enjoyed, but it ended at last. She was wandering restlessly about in the garden while Gene gave Belle her bath when she heard the sound of the cars returning. Somehow it was more than she could do to stay here and greet them smilingly, and she hurried inside and shut herself up in her room. She'd change into something dressy for dinner, she thought. That might cheer her up a little and she didn't care if Ryan's eyebrows went up to the cciling, or if Debra did remark scathingly as she had once before, "Pretty!"

She heard the others come upstairs, heard doors opening and closing as the shower was used and they went into their rooms to change. Then, after a short silence, somebody tapped on her door. Ryan, she thought automatically, her heart beginning to beat a wild tattoo. But of course it wouldn't be Ryan, he was too busy these days with Debra to be bothering about Ashleigh Stevens.

"Come in," she called, expecting Gene, or even Belle.

The door opened and Ryan looked in. Then seeing she was fully dressed—in a violet-and-blue concoction with a scooped, frill-trimmed neckline—he pushed the door wider and came into the room.

"How about coming out of hiding, Ashleigh?" His eyes moved over her slowly, taking in the cloud of dark hair that she'd been brushing, the faint pink in her cheeks caused by the mere sight of him, the downcast lashes as she tried to avoid those startlingly blue eyes of his.

"I'm not in hiding," she said coolly. "I'll be ready in a minute."

"Then make it a short minute," he said. "We're all gathering downstairs on the verandah and we're about to open a bottle of champagne."

Ashleigh's eyes widened with shock, just as though she hadn't been expecting something like this. She leaned back against the dressing table, her throat dry. So it had happened at last. The engagement. And—oh God—she still had to ask Debra about getting a lift to Darwin. She wished she'd got it over before, because now she could just see Ryan smiling sardonically, as if to tell her that she'd been playing a losing game all along.

"What's the occasion?" she asked, as if she didn't know. "Something to do with the border muster?"

"No. An engagement," he said.

"Yours," she wanted to say but the word stuck in her throat. She felt dizzy, sick. She wanted to throw herself face down on the bed and cry. But she didn't of course. With a superhuman effort, she turned back to the mirror, picked up her brush again, and drew it through her hair.

"I should have guessed," she said coolly, looking at him through the glass.

She went on brushing her hair and refused to look at him, afraid of what he might read in her eyes.

"You don't sound over-enthusiastic," he remarked and she shrugged.

"Why would I be? I'm just passing through. It doesn't matter to me who marries who."

"Doesn't it? Are you quite sure of that?"

Suddenly his hand was on her shoulder and he'd swung her round from the mirror, compelling her to look at him. His eyes were smouldering and she felt a flame leap up inside her. Her flesh burned where his fingers touched it, and her bones were melting. She half closed her eyes and swayed towards him as everything but this man, this moment were wiped from her mind as if by magic. Her hairbrush slipped from her hand, falling to the carpeted floor with a soft thud, and Ryan drew her to him fiercely, demandingly. She was aware of him in every nerve as his arms closed around her and their bodies made warm, intimate contact from breast to thigh. Her head fell back and she parted her lips to his kisses, a surge of pure pleasure filling her being as though she were a goblet being filled with wine. It was like that day under the paper-barks, it was like coming back to an Eden dreamed of and half forgotten. . . .

It wasn't until his mouth left hers so they could both draw a breath that she began to realise, at first dimly and then with stultifying clarity, just what she was doing: abandoning herself shamelessly to a man who'd just told her he was engaged to another woman. How could she? How could *he*? What sort of a man was he that he could play with her so cruelly, cashing in on his assurance that she found him sexually irresistible? And he was so right—she did find him that. . . . She drew a shuddering breath and thrust him away.

"Let me alone! You told me once you had some moral standards even if I didn't," she said tremblingly. "So just—prove it, will you? I don't know what you want of me and I—I don't care. But don't touch me in future. Don't *touch* me. Do you understand?"

His hands, that had been lingering softly on her waist, fell away from her abruptly and his eyes hardened, their colour even more startlingly blue as the pupils contracted to mere pinpoints.

"Yes—I understand. You make yourself very clear, Ashleigh. . . . I apologise. I assure you it won't happen again." His voice, in contrast with hers, was reasonable and steady, and as he finished speaking, he turned away and strode across to the door. From there he looked back at her to say curtly, "Come down as soon as you can. I don't want the fun spoiled for Betty-Lou and David."

Ashleigh stared at him, her eyes widening as she tried to take in what he was saying. Betty-Lou and David! Her mouth was dry and she seemed incapable of speech, and before she could pull herself together, he was gone.

With a little moan, she staggered to the bed and collapsed on it. She wanted to laugh hysterically, she wanted to cry. Betty-Lou and David! Love certainly came quickly in the outback! And she'd taken it for granted it was Ryan and Debra who were announcing their engagement.

A few tears escaped from under her lids and ran down the side of her face. If only she'd known! Yet what difference would it make in the long run, she thought futilely. David and Betty-Lou this evening, Ryan and Debra perhaps tomorrow. So she was glad she'd put him in his place. She had to be glad, or she was out of her mind.

She jumped up from the bed, brushing away her tears angrily. He thought he could do as he liked with her: twist her round his little finger, play with her, then turn his back. But this time she'd been the one to turn her back and she was going to keep it that way.

When she went downstairs to the verandah a few minutes later, her nerves were quivering and she hoped it wasn't noticeable. At least she was able to smile and to kiss Betty-Lou and congratulate her and David, who both looked as pleased as though they'd won a million dollars.

Ryan, who was busy with the champagne, barely gave her a glance, to her relief. Crystal champagne glasses had been set out on a gleaming silver tray, and there were platters of little savoury biscuits, nuts, and olives. Everyone looked pleased and happy, and Belle, dancing around in her pink pyjamas, her eyes bright, added a family touch that somehow made Ashleigh aware that she was the one outsider.

She met Ryan's eyes only once, when he handed her a glass of champagne, and she managed to look cool. Though not as cool as he looked, she thought, her heart shaking in spite of herself. The conversation was very much family style, and Ashleigh didn't take much of it in. She heard Colin say jokingly that he wasn't going to let his young brother beat him to the altar and she saw Debra toss Ryan an intimate look that seemed to suggest that *they* had a surprise in store for everyone. Perhaps they were keeping their announcement until later so as not to steal the other couple's thunder.

When the champagne was finished, the men went into the garden to get the barbecue ready, and Gene, with Betty-Lou in tow, whisked off to the kitchen to see about a salad. Ashleigh was left alone with Debra, who leaned against the verandah rail and lit a cigarette. Ashleigh loaded the glasses onto the tray and was trying to make up her mind to ask the other girl about giving her a lift to Darwin when Debra spoke drawlingly.

"What's bothering you, Ashleigh? You look as sad as a cow that's lost her calf. Wishing you were in Darwin with Don, I suppose, instead of out of your element here."

Ashleigh flushed faintly. She'd sooner Debra thought that than anything else, but it still didn't make her like her rather patronising tone.

"I didn't know I looked so gloomy," she said, summoning a smile. "As a matter of fact, I was going to ask you if you'd mind giving me a lift to Darwin when you go. I don't know how long it's going to be before the car's fixed and—"

"And you've had enough of the outback," Debra supplied, ashing her cigarette in a nearby pot plant. "You haven't been enjoying yourself much, have you, you poor thing? You're like a fish out of water here. Well, I did have a premonition you wouldn't take to the Kimberleys exactly as if it were your element."

But I have, Ashleigh wanted to retort, irritated by the other girl's attitude. However, she let it pass, and asked mildly, *"Can* you give me a lift? You'll be leaving in a couple of days, won't you?"

Debra let her glance trail over Ashleigh's blue-and-mauve dress, and then absent-mindedly smoothed a hand over her hip, its curve sleekly outlined by the pale beige pants she wore with a long-sleeved blouse of white-and-tan striped silk. Ashleigh was quite sure it wasn't intentional, but it did seem to emphasise the inappropriateness of her own attire to the outback.

"I'd love to help you out, Ashleigh. I can see you're just itching to be on your way, but I don't know when I'll be leaving. In fact," she concluded, "it's quite likely Don's car will be ready before I am."

Ashleigh listened frowningly. Don had been so sure Debra was only staying a week; but of course, she could easily change her plans, once she was engaged to Ryan. And Ashleigh was convinced that would be any day now.

"Never mind," she murmured, and Debra said bracingly, "You'll just have to grin and bear it, Ashleigh. But cheer up, I'm sure after this you'll find Darwin quite acceptable. And when you're out on safari you'll be with Don, which will be a very different kettle of fish, won't it? Someone of your very own to look after you."

"Yes," Ashleigh said, seething just slightly and quite unjustifiably and glad when at that moment Gene and Betty-Lou came onto the verandah, each carrying a platter of salad.

"There's a pile of sliced bread in the kitchen, Ashleigh," Gene said gaily. "You wouldn't like to butter it, would you?"

"Of course I would." Ashleigh disappeared to the kitchen, leaving Debra to go down to the barbecue—and the men—with the other two girls.

She buttered the bread and tried to ignore the tears that kept coming to her eyes and to tell herself they were because she was going to have to grin and bear it, as Debra had put it, for a few days longer than she'd hoped.

Before they broke up the celebrations that night, a picnic to the Crystal Pool was arranged for the next day. Ashleigh searched desperately for an excuse not to go, but there was none, because even Gene was enthusiastic.

"I'm always willing to celebrate an engagement in the family," Ashleigh heard her remark, and then tell Ryan lightly, "you'll be next, Ryan. I'll be sorry I've said I'd go to Perth, with all the fun and games going on here."

"It'll do you good, Gene," Ryan said.

Gene replied jokingly, "I mightn't come back, you know. I shan't be needed."

"Needed or not, you know you're always welcome here," he said hugging her.

It gave Ashleigh a curious feeling to see the affection between the brother and sister. Gene had said once that Ryan had a soft heart, and she knew that it wasn't as hard as she liked to imagine. With those he loved, he could be warm and affectionate and kind. But not towards her.

As she went up to bed that night, she felt very much an outsider, a ring in, who had no business being here at all. Ryan had said Gene had invited her to stay, but it wasn't as simple as that. She'd try to earn her keep, she thought, as she lay in the darkness. She'd make sure she wasn't a free-loader. She'd help Gene all she could. There'd be extra meals to prepare and somehow she didn't think Debra would be giving a hand in the kitchen. And Betty-Lou would probably have most of her time taken up by David.

She was filled with apprehension when she got up the next morning. The thought of going back to the Crystal Pool sent waves of troubled emotions surging through her, and she wished she didn't have to go through with it.

However, as it turned out, she needn't have worried. She didn't even have to travel in the same car as Ryan, and when they reached the pool, instead of going into the water with the others for a swim, she chose to stay with Gene and get the picnic laid out. Belle hadn't come, because it was Josh's birthday—he was five—and she was spending the day with the Grays. The two women had a pleasant time together, and Ashleigh deliberately took no interest in what the others were doing. She definitely didn't want to know whether Debra and Ryan had wandered off on their own.

As they came trailing back for lunch, she noticed that Debra, in her trim dark-green swimsuit, looked unexpectedly thin, and that her permed hair was frizzy from its soaking. Yet even thin and frizzy-haired, she was an attractive girl, and obviously Ryan thought so too. All his attention was for her, and she was loving it.

Ashleigh, of course, was not.

After lunch, they all trooped off to see the bowerbird's playground, to Betty-Lou's delight, and then David suggested that, instead of staying where they were, they should go the long way home via the billabong, where there were lashings of birds to be seen. The suggestion met with general approval.

Colin and Ashleigh helped Gene pack up and the other four went ahead in Ryan's car.

"You'll like the billabong," Colin told Ashleigh, beside him in the front seat as they set off a few minutes later. "There are more birds there than at the pool. Water-lilies too. Very pretty. . . . I'm for another swim, myself. I could do with a bit of a cool-down. How about you girls joining me?"

Gene shuddered. "Not me. I'm a hopeless swimmer and I'm always scared there'll be crocodiles in those murky waters."

"Oh, I haven't seen a croc there for years," Colin said laconically, as he turned the car off the track and headed towards a thick belt of timber. "We often swim in the billabong when we're mustering this paddock and we've never had any bother. If there were any crocs, they'd be the little freshwater Johnstons, anyhow. And they're only interested in fish, not in big hunks of flesh like me and Dave."

"I'm still not interested," Gene said firmly, and Ashleigh had a feeling she wasn't interested either.

When they pulled up near the other car under the paper-barks a few minutes later, David and Ryan were already in their swimming trunks and on their way to the water, and in the car, Debra and Betty-Lou were busily stripping off their shirts and pants and presently appeared in their swimsuits.

"We're going to take a swim," Betty-Lou said, as the two of them came over to the car. "It's so darned hot. Are you coming?"

"I am," Colin said with alacrity. He got out of the car and disappeared to change. Ashleigh looked doubtfully at the great expanse of water beyond the trees, then realised Debra was watching her with a knowing smile.

"I can see the billabong doesn't attract you, Ashleigh. Too muddy. You're used to the nice clean sand and the Indian Ocean at Cottesloe, aren't you? Well, let's go, Betty-Lou."

They walked off, without giving Ashleigh a chance to answer, and she felt herself fuming. She was used to Cottesloe, and she couldn't pretend the billabong attracted her, but she wasn't such a softie that she wouldn't swim there. If Betty-Lou was game, then so was she.

"I'm going in," she told Gene, and proceeded to get out of her clothes and into her bikini.

"You won't stay in that water for long," Gene predicted. "Why don't you just have a wander round and watch the birds?"

"I'll do that later," Ashleigh said.

By the time she was ready, the others were all in the water. The men appeared to be having a race to the other side of the billabong, which was quite a distance, but Betty-Lou and Debra were splashing about not far from the shore.

Somehow she didn't feel like joining them, particularly in her pink-and-cinnamon bikini that was definitely out of place in this setting. Instead, she walked along the shore a little way and stood shading her eyes and looking at a patch of exquisite water-lilies, the long-stemmed flowers, some blue, some white, standing up above the great flat leaves and reminding her of long-legged birds. Red dragon-flies, their wings glistening in the sun, darted and hung above them, and the soft shadows of the overhanging paper-barks made the whole scene look very romantic.

But when she found a clear place to enter the water, it decidedly didn't look romantic. And she *was* squeamish, going into that murky water. However, she was going to prove something to Debra Davis if it killed her.

Smoothly, with hardly a splash, she struck out for the centre of the billabong. The Langton men were still somewhere over there, and as well there was a flotilla of pelicans sailing along majestically. She wouldn't swim right across, because Ryan would be sure to think she was chasing him, but neither was she going to play about in the shallows. That wouldn't prove anything to Debra, or to herself.

After awhile, rather surprisingly, she forgot about the murkiness and began to enjoy herself. In the middle of the billabong, she trod water and watched the rainbow birds swooping on insects. As well, there was a darter diving for fish, and she watched in fascination as it emerged, then perched on a dead branch, its dark wings extended to dry.

She'd turned around and was swimming slowly back towards the shore when she heard a shriek and saw Betty-Lou and Debra splash out of the water. On the bank they turned to watch her. Betty-Lou was gesticulating frantically, but Ashleigh hadn't the faintest idea what it was all about. She stopped swimming and trod water, staring around her, looking for whatever it was that was exciting Betty-Lou. At first she saw nothing and then she caught sight of a log floating towards her.

A log? Or was it—something else?

Oh God! It was a crocodile!

She was petrified. Her heart pounded so hard she thought it would burst, and she didn't know why she didn't sink. Some instinct seemed to keep her afloat, and she tried desperately to think what she should do. But she hadn't the faintest notion. In any case, she was so scared she was incapable of action.

It's only a freshwater crocodile, whispered a voice somewhere inside her head, as the log glided nearer and nearer. They eat fish, not people. No crocodile in its right mind would ever mistake you for a fish . . .

Seconds—or was it hours?—later, the crocodile drifted past. It was only a few feet away and it wasn't very big, but she saw with startling clarity its nostrils, its eyes, its horny skin, the gentle swishing of its tail that was its way of swimming . . .

At some stage after that, she began to move, to swim slowly, steadily, towards the shore, as if nothing at all had happened. It was purely mechanical, as if her body, though it was swamped with fear, knew what must be done and did it, without any direction from her.

Presently, without really knowing how she got there, she discovered she was standing on the muddy bank. Trembling, feeling as if she were about to collapse, she squeezed the water out of her hair.

Betty-Lou and Debra and Gene appeared, and the American girl exclaimed with a laugh, "Ashleigh! Weren't you scared? Debra and I just about died of fright when we saw that crocodile cruising along. We couldn't get out of the water fast enough."

Ashleigh's lips parted but she couldn't speak. What

she wanted most was to burst into tears, to have someone fold their arms around her and comfort her, and kiss her.

But no one was going to comfort her, let alone kiss her, and they all began to walk back towards the cars, Ashleigh hoping that her legs would carry her as far as that.

"I've spread out a rug under the trees and there's some nice hot tea in the thermos," Gene said soothingly. "I guess you'd like some, Ashleigh. And here come the boys," she added. "They're probably wondering what all the panic was about."

"Panic?" Debra said. "All Betty-Lou and I did was use our heads and get out of the way. Poor Ashleigh didn't even know what it was all about. *I* knew it was a Johnston and wouldn't eat her, but if *she'd* known there was a croc around she'd have bounded out of the water like a kangaroo."

Oh no, I wouldn't have, Ashleigh thought. Debra was quite wrong. She'd been too scared to move, let alone jump like a kangaroo. In fact, she was still too shaken to trust her voice. Instead she tried to smile, but had to bite her lip to stop it from trembling.

She was cradling a mug of hot, comforting tea in her hands by the time the men joined them. In spite of the heat of the day, she felt icily cold, yet it seemed just too much to go to the car to get her clothes, or even a towel.

Betty-Lou rushed up to David and threw herself into his arms. "Do you guys realise we were all just about eaten alive by crocodiles?"

No, they didn't, and she began to tell her version of the story, exaggerating everything and getting all the mileage she could out of it, while Debra smiled aloofly, as though it was a lot of fuss about nothing.

And *that* was just a little bit funny, Ashleigh thought, because even if it had been only Betty-Lou who'd screamed, Debra had certainly got out of the water in double-quick time, which was of course the sensible thing to do. She sipped her tea and tried not to shiver, and was suddenly aware that Ryan was looking at her, his eyes narrowed. She felt cold and naked and exposed in her bikini, and she knew her face was ashen. Casually, as if unaware of his regard, she turned away and began to stroll towards the car.

"It didn't *really* come anywhere near us," she heard Betty-Lou admit. "But it sailed right past Ashleigh, and she didn't turn a hair," she concluded with a shudder.

Debra laughed. "Ashleigh thought it was a log, which goes to show that ignorance is bliss. At all events, it was only a harmless little Johnston."

Yes, of course it was, Ashleigh thought, not looking back, pretending she hadn't heard what was being said. It was no use trying to persuade herself she'd been in any danger. She hadn't. Yet all the same, Debra's rather slighting remarks stung, and at the memory of those strangely lidded reptilian eyes, the pebbly nostrils, the horny skin, she felt a renewal of the fear and revulsion she'd felt in the water.

She'd put her tea mug on the ground and was wrapping her towel around her when Ryan left the others and came in her direction. At once, a great lump came into her throat and she longed to run to him the way Betty-Lou had gone to David. She wanted his arms around her, she wanted to—to hang on to him and tell him how frightened she'd been.

She swallowed the lump and picked up her tea mug. He'd gone to the other car, so maybe he wasn't going to take any notice of her after all. That was likely, seeing he'd practically ignored her all day. Why should he care about the incident at the billabong, or even be interested?

But it seemed he wasn't ignoring her now. He took

something from his car and then came straight over to her. Without even raising her head, she knew that he was taking in every shivering, trembling inch of her that was visible outside the pink towel. When he stopped only eighteen inches away, she looked up and found she was staring straight into his brilliantly blue eyes.

He looked back at her wordlessly, a curious expression on his face. Then he reached out and took her cup from her, and she watched dazedly as he poured something into it from a flask.

"Brandy," he said handing it back to her. "Drink it. You need it. You're shaking like a bit of shivery grass, and you look ghastly."

Tears rushed to her eyes and, scarcely knowing what she was doing, she obeyed him, swallowing down the cooling tea into which he'd splashed a generous amount of spirit. It was sweet and fiery, and with the warmth that ran along her veins came another deeper warmth, because he'd noticed her distress, and cared at least a little. . . .

"I'm more sorry than I can say about what happened," he said unsmilingly. "I should never have let you swim in the billabong. Debra knew enough to stay in the shallow water. Oh sure, it was only a little Johnston, but not many people like to go swimming with any sort of a croc. You knew it was there, didn't you? You didn't think it was a log."

"Only at first," she murmured. "I should have got out of the water like the others but my—my limbs just seized up. Like the engine of Don's car," she added with a shaky laugh. "I wasn't brought up in the outback. I was too scared to move."

"All the same, you didn't lose your head. Most girls would have. I had no idea anything was wrong, but God knows what could have happened! I feel very responsible."

"For me? But you're not," she said, surprised more

at the way he was looking at her than at anything else.
His eyes were so warm and grave and caring, almost as
if—

"I am responsible, Ashleigh. At least while you're
here," he said, his voice low. At the same moment, he
took the empty cup from her, and as he set it down on
the ground, she covered her eyes with her hands. She
didn't know why, but she was crying. She felt the tears
run down between her fingers, and then his arms were
around her and he held her close to him, letting her rest
her head on his bare chest, putting his cheek against her
damp hair.

She wept silently and weakly for perhaps a minute,
and then drew a deep breath and made an effort to pull
herself together, thinking of the others . . . wondering
if they were watching. . . .

"I'm all right now. Thank you for the brandy, it's
made me feel better. Hadn't we better go back to the
others? They'll think—"

She broke off. Better not to say what they'd think.
She wiped her eyes swiftly with the back of her hand,
blinking to clear her vision. The others were down
there somewhere, on the rug Gene had spread out
under the trees. She felt ashamed of herself for being so
weak as to go into Ryan's arms. She knew that if she
were Debra, she wouldn't like it one little bit.

"Don't worry," he murmured. "They've all gone to
look at an egret's nest that David says has a couple of
chicks in it." He took her hands and pulled her against
his body with a movement that was gentle but completely inexorable. The pink towel slipped from around
her shoulders, their hips touched, she felt his bare
thighs against her own, and though a minute ago she'd
been just as close to him, this time it was different. She
was acutely conscious of him physically now, and a
whole host of emotions and sensations were creating
havoc in her mind and her body.

She raised her head slowly and looked into his face, wondering what he was thinking. Wondering if he knew what she was thinking about him, about their being together like this. She didn't dare examine her own thoughts too clearly, but let them hover about like the red dragon-flies she'd seen over the water-lilies—never coming to rest anywhere, never still, never clearly visible. She did know one thing of course, and that was that being here with Ryan, having him look at her the way he was doing, feeling the warmth of his body against her own, was the closest thing to heaven she could imagine, though of course it couldn't last.

When his mouth came down to find hers, it seemed right and inevitable and she parted her lips as he kissed her long and drowningly. She felt as she had at the pool that day they'd looked so deeply into each other's eyes. For her there was the same feeling of pleasure, of communication at the deepest level. When his lips parted from hers slowly, lingeringly, she turned her face a little, touching her mouth to his bare skin and tasting it with her tongue. His arms tightened around her, and she heard him groan, as he trailed softly passionate kisses down the side of her neck, and quite suddenly she wondered what on earth she was doing— if the brandy had made her drunk.

"Don't go," he muttered, feeling the sharp but infinitesimal movement she'd made away from him, and helplessly, willingly, she relaxed again. She could hear the hard beating of his heart as she wound her arms around him and moved her body against his. No wildly sexual feelings were tearing her apart, yet she was aware of a languorousness that she knew was equally meaningful. If he chose, he could make her lose her head within seconds. And just a little, she hoped he would.

She'd lifted her face to his and they were kissing again, their lips clinging. Her heart raced and her self-control was beginning to slip when he put her away from him with a gentle but positive movement.

"Here come the others," he said quietly. He twined his fingers tightly in hers and looked down at her intently. "You're all right, aren't you, Ashleigh?"

"Perfectly," she said, her voice quivering. She felt she'd been dragged back from the brink of paradise. She released her fingers from his and picked up her towel, draping it around her body as she began to walk unsteadily ahead of him towards the billabong.

Gene came into sight and the others appeared behind her, Betty-Lou excitedly voluble about the egrets, the brolgas, a pair of jabirus. And while she babbled on, Debra looked through her lashes at Ashleigh, her expression unsmiling and thoughtful.

Ashleigh felt her mouth tremble, as if Ryan's kisses showed on it. With a terrible feeling of guilt, she murmured an excuse and went to the car to dress.

For the rest of the day, she took care to keep away from Ryan.

# Chapter Nine

David and Betty-Lou left the next day. Betty-Lou wanted her uncle and aunt to meet David so that they could write her parents first-hand information about him. Once they'd gone, Ryan and Colin went back to their stock-work, and Ashleigh, alone in the house with Gene and Debra, felt strangely on edge. She didn't know what to make of what had happened at the billabong yesterday. It didn't seem possible that Ryan didn't have the same feeling for her as she had for him, but she couldn't escape from the fact that his intention was to marry Debra. Gene had made that plain enough.

For once she didn't feel like walking down to Selma's with Gene and Belle, and instead she found a book and went onto the verandah, where she made herself comfortable on a lounger and tried to read. But her mind wandered away almost at once—to Ryan, to Debra, to Don, to the way this escapade had led her inexorably into the spot she was in now.

But perhaps she wasn't in a spot at all. All that would happen was that she'd leave Crystal Downs in a few days' time, and that would be the end of the story.

"Not such a good book?" It was Debra, and she dropped down into a chair and looked at Ashleigh smilingly. "I guess you feel like a little peace and quiet after the last few hectic days—though I suppose they haven't been so hectic for you."

"Hectic enough," Ashleigh murmured, and closed the book. She had a feeling Debra hadn't come onto the verandah merely for idle chit-chat, and she was soon proved to be right.

Debra took out cigarettes and lit one. "I know you don't smoke, so I won't offer you one, Ashleigh. Have you recovered from the crocodile incident?"

"Quite," Ashleigh said, flushing a little. Debra made it sound as if she'd really made a fuss, and she was quite sure she hadn't.

"I saw Ryan comforting you, by the way, but I didn't interrupt," Debra went on dryly, and Ashleigh's slightly flushed face turned scarlet. "I don't know what you made of his attentions, but I wouldn't take them too seriously. He's very soft-hearted when it comes to tears. You've possibly seen him with Belle."

She stopped and drew on her cigarette and Ashleigh couldn't think of a thing to say. In any case, she didn't want to talk to Debra about Ryan.

"You haven't changed your mind about Don, I hope," Debra said, when she was silent. Her grey eyes examined Ashleigh with a cool look that refused to accept evasion.

Ashleigh looked back at her equally coolly. "I'm sorry, but I don't recollect discussing Don with you," she said, and was careful to smile as she spoke.

Debra made a face. "No. But Don's been quite open about your relationship. And I heard from Caryl that you were keeping your engagement quiet because your family wasn't over-keen, or something like that." She studied her cigarette for a moment, then looked up, her eyes bright. "That's your business of course, but Ryan is my business, because I happen to want to marry him."

Ashleigh felt a shock go through her. It was something she already knew, but to hear it said like that shook her. She bit her lip and wished she'd stuck to Gene; then this conversation could never have taken place.

"Of course I'm aware Ryan is a little bemused by you," Debra said softly. "And I think I know why. There's a wide-eyed look about you that's very reminiscent of the girl he married in his early twenties. I knew Christine quite well and I can see it myself. I saw it the minute I met you, in fact, in Broome. It's unsettled Ryan, but it won't last. It can't. It's too unrealistic and he has too much sense. Once you're out of his orbit, he'll put you out of his mind very quickly."

Listening, Ashleigh felt sick. Was that true? Was that why Ryan was drawn to her, as she knew very well he was? Gene had already remarked that she shared some quality with Christine, so it was possible. It was more than coincidence that two people had seen a resemblance, and she wished futilely that she'd never allowed herself to dream, to hope. To Ryan she was just an insubstantial shadow, a girl who evoked his nostalgic past . . .

"So you see," Debra said, watching her reaction and tossing her cigarette butt over the verandah rail, "you'd be very silly to let Ryan get under your skin. You stick to Don, Ashleigh. He loves you for what you are."

Ashleigh managed a shrug—a purely reflex action that had something to do with salvaging her pride. "I think you're making mountains out of molehills,

Debra. In fact, I don't really know what you're talking about. Are you sure you aren't getting over-anxious because Ryan hasn't asked you to marry him?"

Debra shot her an icy look and her mouth tightened.

"It's you I'm anxious about," she snapped. "I just wanted to warn you not to lose your head. Your behaviour's been rather pathetic, you know." She jumped to her feet. "I'm going out to catch up with the men; Ryan suggested it. I'll see you at dinner. Think about what I've said, won't you?" she added as she walked off.

Ashleigh did think about it, not only about what Debra had said, but about what Ryan had not said. Out at the billabong yesterday, although he'd kissed her, looked into her eyes as if she were really special, as if he felt exactly the way she did, what *had* he said? Nothing. Yes, when she really thought back, there'd been nothing said at all. It was no wonder she'd been unable to make sense of his behaviour. It was like reading a book and turning the page to find it ended in the middle of a sentence. What Debra had said explained it all very neatly. His relationship with Ashleigh—such as it was —was no more than a dream journey back into the past. . . .

That night at the dinner table, she tried hard to keep her eyes from straying to Ryan, sure that every time she looked at him, spoke to him, Debra was taking it in and finding her behaviour pathetic. As it was, she thought bitterly. Really pathetic. Imagine the idiocy of being stranded on a cattle station and falling in love with the boss. So who was the dreamer? With a determined effort, she dragged her attention back to the conversation. It was about camp horses, a subject about which she knew nothing, while Debra was able not only to listen intelligently, but to put in a comment of her own now and again.

"Speaking as one who merely watches," she was now remarking brightly, "I get the idea that mares make the best camp horses. Is that right?"

"As a general rule, yes," Colin agreed. "But that little mare Jimmy's so keen on will never make a good camp horse. You might have noticed this afternoon—it watches the steer all right, but there's nothing of the ballet dancer about it when it comes to turning. It's as clumsy as a clown."

Ashleigh felt Ryan's glance move to her face, and she looked back at him, unable to help herself, taking in the blueness of his eyes, the hardness of his jawline, the mobility of his mouth. Liking—loving—everything that she saw. But what did he feel about what *he* saw? His eyes were warm, but she couldn't understand their warmth and she dropped her lashes. She didn't like the idea of being identified with a girl who was dead. Abruptly, she got up from the table and went to help Gene with the coffee.

There was a lull in the conversation as they handed it around, and Gene remarked, "Now I can get a word in. I'd like a volunteer to drive me and Belle to Kununurra in the next day or so to catch the plane. I want to do some shopping before the wedding. Belle's grown out of all her clothes, and I definitely need something new or I won't be the sensation I'm hoping to be. So what about it?"

She looked from one to the other of her two brothers, and after the fraction of a second Ryan said, "We're pretty busy at the moment what with one thing and another. The best thing will be for you to go with Debra. You'll get a better flight from Darwin, in any case." He glanced at Debra. "You have to get back to work soon, don't you, Debra?"

Debra didn't answer immediately. Colin had leaned forward to light a cigarette for her, and she drew on it slowly, her eyes narrowed. She was wearing plain silver earrings and she looked very attractive in a straight white dress with her favourite mandarin collar.

"I don't actually have a specific deadline," she said then. "But if I can help out, then of course I shall. Just name the day you want to leave, Gene, and I'll be ready."

"Well then—how about the day after tomorrow?" Gene suggested. "Or is that too soon for you?"

Debra's glance slid quickly to Ryan and then to her cigarette as she ashed it carefully. "Not at all. Just whenever you say."

"Then that's settled," Ryan said. "I know you don't want to spend all that much longer here, Debra. You have an interesting assignment waiting for you when you go home, don't you? In Bali, I understand."

"Yes. Balinese village life, from the woman's angle," Debra agreed with a bright smile. "I haven't altogether made up my mind to do it, though. The photographer on the job's a man whose company I can do without, and though it's definitely tempting, I could be persuaded to pass it up."

She looked directly at Ryan as she spoke and he looked back at her. With a feeling of embarrassment, Ashleigh stared down at her empty cup. That sounded like a very broad hint, but if Ryan was going to persuade Debra to pass up her assignment in Bali, it didn't seem he was going to do it now.

She helped Gene carry the dishes out to the kitchen and stack them in the sink, and when they went out to the verandah, enticed by the sound of Colin strumming away at his guitar, it was to find him alone. Debra and Ryan had disappeared and Ashleigh felt sick with jealousy.

Debra's going meant that she'd have to leave too, of course. She'd asked for a lift, and she didn't imagine Debra would have forgotten it. The sooner she was out of the way, the sooner Ryan would come back to his senses; that was probably how Debra saw it.

So for her it was the end of the adventure. It was time to go back to her own life and her own problems: what to do about Don, about her future. She knew now she couldn't marry Don, and neither was she going back to Perth to be wrapped up in cotton wool again. She thought of Debra's assignment in Bali and wished she were equipped to do something like that. But she wasn't equipped for anything. In this age of women's lib, Ashleigh Stevens was a misfit, a throwback, a girl who'd give anything just to be a wife—but not to anyone at all; to Ryan Langton. . . .

"How's the packing going, Ashleigh?" Debra asked at dinner the next night. The men had been out all day and Debra had been out too. She hadn't spoken to Ashleigh about coming to Darwin with her, but she obviously took it for granted that she would.

"I haven't started yet," Ashleigh murmured, her heart hammering. She hadn't even told Ryan or Gene that she was going. She'd meant to do it sometime tonight, but the fact was, she hadn't been looking forward to it.

"You'd better get it done before you go to bed," Debra warned. "We'll be leaving early in the morning." She turned back to Colin and Ryan. "You men will be all on your own tomorrow. Ashleigh's tired of waiting around, she wants to get back to her fiancé. Don't you, Ashleigh?"

Ashleigh felt a pulse beating at her temples. She didn't want to get back to Don, and he wasn't her fiancé, but it might be better if Ryan, and everyone else, thought he was. She fiddled with her wine glass— red wine tonight to go with the steak and a special dinner because "goodness knows when we'll all be together again, if ever," Gene had said.

"So you and Don are actually engaged, are you,

Ashleigh?" Ryan's words broke in on her thoughts. "You've kept very quiet about it. I didn't know it was official."

"It's not," Debra put in before Ashleigh could speak. "Ashleigh's people don't altogether approve. I don't know why. I like Don, and Caryl and Len have a lot of time for him. They say this safari thing should go with a swing when he takes over. He has money to put into it, which they haven't."

Don had money to put into it? That was the first Ashleigh had heard of it. In fact, she knew from Laura that he'd had to go to a lot of trouble to get a loan to buy the business. Unwillingly, she thought of the things Esme had said about Don, insinuating that he was interested in the money that would come to Ashleigh when she married. She hadn't believed it before, but now it seemed there could be at least a grain of truth in it. It wasn't a pleasant thought.

Immediately after dinner, she went upstairs to pack. Debra had said they'd make an early start as she didn't want to stop anywhere overnight, and as Ashleigh folded her clothes, she tried to anaesthetise her mind— not to think of Ryan. Once she'd left here, she'd never see any of them again; it would all disappear in a puff of smoke.

She was feeling very low when someone knocked on the door and she called an automatic but shaky, "Come in," then stiffened as Ryan appeared. He came right into the room and stood looking down at her, his eyes veiled and uncommunicative.

Self-consciously she pushed her dark hair back from her face and looked back at him warily. Had he come to say good bye? She didn't know if she could stand it. Even now, she longed to reach out, to touch him.

"What do you want?" she asked huskily.

His eyebrows rose quizzically and his glance went to

her mouth. "You didn't tell me you were running off with Debra—back to your fiancé."

"No . . . I'm sorry. I—I meant to tell you but you were out all day."

"Why the rush?" he asked after a moment, and her face flamed.

"I've been here too long already. I should never have stayed in the first place. Don doesn't want me to wait for the car now. He said he'd arrange some other way of getting it to Darwin."

He looked at her levelly. "Well, that doesn't suit me. If you'd let me know what was in your mind, I'd have told you that Charlie's due home tomorrow. You'll wait for the car. I've already explained to Debra, and I'm sure your fiancé will understand."

Her fiancé. "We're not—" she began and he finished for her, "Not officially engaged? I didn't really think you were." As he looked at her, his expression changed. An undisguised look of hunger came over his face and she more than half-expected him to seize hold of her and take her in his arms. But he didn't, and she wished she could read what was in his mind. Perhaps it was beginning to dawn on him that this impulse he had towards her was worth nothing.

Suddenly, unable to help herself, she asked tremblingly, "Why do you look at me like that? Is it because I remind you of Christine?"

She saw shock, then anger, in his face.

"What in *hell* are you talking about? Who's been putting ideas like that into your head?"

"People," she said, her voice low. "Is it true?"

"No, it's not true." A nerve twitched at the angle of his jaw. With a feeling she'd intruded where she had no right to intrude, Ashleigh took an armful of clothes from her open suitcase and crossed the room with them to the dressing table. When she glanced up, she saw in the mirror that he was still looking at her.

"Perhaps you do remind me of her," he said quietly. And then he turned and left the room.

She stood perfectly still for what seemed a long time. What had he meant? And what did it matter?

Moving like an automaton, she began to unpack her clothes again, which was probably a waste of time. If Charlie were coming home tomorrow, then she'd soon be on her way—and facing the ordeal of driving alone to Darwin. Well, independence was what she'd wanted and that was what she was getting, and she wasn't going to crumple up and cry, she thought, mentally straightening her shoulders.

She dressed and went downstairs very early next morning so she could say good bye to Gene and Belle and Debra. She'd had no trouble waking, she'd slept so badly. The others had had their breakfast, and though Colin had gone, Ryan was still there, dressed for a working day in fawn shirt and tough drill pants.

The luggage was being loaded into Debra's car, and Ashleigh hurried outside. She could imagine how unhappy the other girl would be about leaving her here with Ryan, and she didn't like it herself one little bit. Yet what could she do about it? With Charlie returning today, it would be plain stupidity not to wait for the car. That was the only reason she was staying and she hoped Debra realised it.

The morning air was cool, and fleeting clouds drifted across the pale sky. Belle was dashing about excitedly, clutching Missie to her, a mixture of tearfulness and self-importance, and Ashleigh saw the tender, loving look on Ryan's face as he picked her up and hugged her and walked slowly to the car with Gene.

Debra waited for Ashleigh.

"So you're not coming with us."

"No. Charlie will be back today, so there's no point."

"I suppose not," Debra said. She raised her voice a little. "Any messages for Don?"

"Will you be seeing him?" Ashleigh asked in surprise.

"Why not? It won't take me much out of my way to call in. We live in the same part of Darwin—in Nakara."

"Oh—then if you'd just let him know the car will be ready in a couple of days. And give him my love," she added with a smile. She'd said it for Debra's benefit, but suddenly discovered that both Gene and Ryan had heard what she'd said and blushed crimson.

Gene made a rueful face, a half humourous reminder of her opinion of Don. As she kissed Ashleigh good bye, she told her, "Don't do anything rash, will you, Ashleigh? You're much too nice a person to go marrying the wrong man. . . . I've enjoyed your company. I only wish you were staying on to look after my big, helpless brothers."

"Oh dear," Debra put in. "I'm sure poor Ashleigh feels she's been here too long already. And your big brothers are far from helpless. If I thought otherwise, I'd drop you and Belle off in Kununurra and come back to look after them myself. How long do you expect to be away?"

"That depends on a lot of things," Gene said. "I don't intend to make this my home permanently, you know."

Ryan opened the car door for Debra and kissed her good bye before she got in. They spoke to each other, but all Ashleigh heard was Debra's cheerful sounding, "I'll see you in Darwin, Ryan."

The car moved off and Ashleigh stood waving until it was out of sight. Suddenly she was super conscious of the fact that she was alone with Ryan.

"You'd better go in and have some breakfast, Ashleigh," he said casually. "I'm going out to see what's happening in the paddocks. Charlie will be home some time this morning, and he'll start work on your car as soon as he can."

"Thank you," she murmured, walking back along the drive beside him and not looking up.

"I hope you can fill in the day on your own. Don't bother about dinner. Colin and I will have a good midday meal with the men. . . . I'll see you tonight."

He left her at the foot of the steps, and she went slowly into the empty house, where she didn't belong. She almost wished she were in that car heading for Darwin instead of here at Crystal Downs, with Ryan coming home to dinner tonight. Almost, but somehow not quite, which was irrational.

She had some breakfast, tidied her room, and then went into the garden, where she cut some flowers to take to Selma, thinking she might like them to welcome her mother-in-law.

She found Selma in the kitchen baking, while Josh was perched on a stool, consoling himself for Belle's departure by making a little loaf "for Nanna." Adam and Paula were doing their lessons on the verandah and making occasional forays to the kitchen for help.

"Charlie's mother's a darling," Selma told Ashleigh after she'd admired the flowers and found some vases for her to put them in. "The kids love her. I don't suppose she'll stay with us more than a few weeks, but it will help her adjust to being without Pop. All her friends are in Port Hedland, and she's taken up bowls recently." She glanced at her watch. "They should be here any time now. I'll have to dash in and tidy myself. You'll be glad when Charlie can get to work on that car won't you? Ryan said it's to have first priority. We'll miss you, you know."

"I'll miss you too," Ashleigh admitted, and really meant it. She finished arranging the flowers; admired

Josh's loaf; told Paula, who was writing a composition, how to spell "billabong;" and then went back to the homestead, not wanting to intrude on the family reunion.

The house-girls had tidied the kitchen and the bedrooms, washed the sheets, and gone, and the house was empty and silent. Ashleigh found a book and went onto the verandah, but her mind was too full of other things for reading. She'd heard a car and knew Charlie was back home, and suddenly the time for her own departure seemed terribly close. She thought of the thousand-odd kilometres she was going to have to drive to Darwin. It would be a challenge, a way of proving something to herself: that she, Ashleigh Stevens, could handle the experience. And she could. She'd changed since she left Perth and her over-protective aunt and uncle. Even the crocodile incident seemed to have proved something. She hadn't been exactly brave, but at least, as Ryan had said, she hadn't lost her head.

But she wasn't going to start thinking of Ryan, and she'd returned to her book when the sound of a plane took her to the verandah rail. Shading her eyes, she saw that it was preparing to come down on the station air-strip. It was a small Beechcraft, of the type they used at the mining company where her uncle was a director. The same as the plane Milton Wade had been flying when she'd persuaded him to take her up with him, before Esme and Walter put a stop to it. That sort of thing wouldn't happen now, she thought. She'd grown up; she simply wouldn't take it.

The plane was coming down to land, and a haze of red dust over the track that was hidden by trees showed that someone—probably Charlie—was going out to meet it.

Feeling vaguely uneasy, Ashleigh went through the house to the kitchen to make herself a pot of tea and a sandwich for lunch. She was carrying the loaded tray back to the verandah when a car pulled up outside, a door slammed, she heard a man's voice, and then, as the car drove off, someone came up the steps.

Ashleigh set the tray down and turned round, her eyes widening with shock. It was Walter!

She moved forward to meet him, her feeling of affection mixed with dread. If he was planning to take her back to Perth, she wasn't going, but she felt her resolve weaken fractionally at the sight of him, so completely out of place here with his hard, intelligent businessman's face, his city clothes. He was carrying the coat of his lightweight suit and had loosened his tie and the collar of his white shirt.

"Uncle!" she exclaimed, kissing him. "What a surprise to see you here! Give me your coat—sit down—I've just made some tea. I'll get another cup."

"Thank you." He looked at her thoughtfully as if somehow he'd expected her to act differently, and Ashleigh realised that she'd changed since she saw him last, become more positive, more self-assured, less inclined to accept his authority. "You're looking well, Ashleigh, and very much at home. I must admit it's not what I'd expected. But—er—where is everyone? You're not here on your own—"

"No of course not, but there's no one else at home at present. The—the girls went out early this morning and the men are working. . . . I shan't be a moment."

She hurried out to the kitchen, feeling a little guilty at having stretched the truth more than somewhat, but knowing that Walter would definitely not approve of her being here alone with two men. And it was all too complicated to explain. She didn't think she need wonder why he was here. Obviously, he'd come to take her back to Perth. But she wasn't going to meekly do as she was told.

When she came back onto the verandah, he'd taken a chair and was looking about him, taking everything in.

As she poured the tea and handed it to him he remarked, "I don't know if you realise it, Ashleigh, but Esme's been worried to death about you. You haven't sent her a word since you left home, and when she rang the Harrises for news, she found that Laura was back and that you were stranded somewhere in the Kimberleys. Do you think it's fair to upset your aunt this way?"

No, Ashleigh supposed it wasn't fair, but for heaven's sake, was she expected to send a daily account of her doings to her aunt, at her age?

"I'm sorry," she said briefly. "But I wish Esme would realise I'm quite capable of managing my own life now."

His eyebrows rose. "Are you?" He refused the sandwiches she offered. "I doubt it. You seem to have gotten yourself into quite a nasty predicament, in fact. If you'd kept in touch, I'd have sent someone to fetch you home immediately."

Yes. Ashleigh knew he'd have done that, and that was exactly why she hadn't let him know. She said firmly, "I didn't want you to do that, Uncle."

He shot her a frowning look. "The mechanic who picked me up at the air-strip just now told me you're going to drive Don Harris's car to Darwin, when he's done some work on it. I can't imagine you're looking forward to doing that—or that you're capable of it, either. It's a risky undertaking for a girl, to say the least of it. I know Don Harris has injured his leg, but just the same, if he had any consideration for you he'd have made other arrangements about his car. In fact, I think you'd better forget all about it and come back home with me."

He was so reasonable that Ashleigh felt trapped. She had to remind herself that she'd be smothered if she went back to Perth, and she shook her head determinedly.

"I'm sorry, Uncle, but I'm not going back to Perth. I have other plans."

Walter's mouth tightened. "Now what silly ideas are you getting into your head, Ashleigh? You won't find work in Darwin, I can assure you of that. If you want to be independent, then the best thing you can do is to accumulate a little more experience in the business world. We'll talk about that later. Meanwhile you'd better run along and pack your bags and hurry up about it. I don't have all day to waste."

Ashleigh's patience suddenly deserted her, and her common sense along with it. She simply was not going to be treated as a child any more.

"I'm getting too old to be spoken to like that, Uncle," she exclaimed vehemently. "I want to make my own decisions. I'm almost twenty—I'm old enough to marry—and that's what I'm going to do. So don't try to order me about." She stopped abruptly, wondering what had got into her to make her say that, and aware that Walter's face had gone red with anger.

"Are you telling me you're going to marry Don Harris?" he exploded. "I don't care how old you are, Ashleigh, I refuse to permit it. If you had an atom of sense you'd know he has his eye on your money. He's practically spent it already, from what I've learned of his doings."

"I'm not going to marry Don Harris," Ashleigh retorted, her face red too.

"I certainly hope you mean that. But I assure you I'm not leaving you in this part of the world to drift around aimlessly and get yourself into more trouble. And if it's not Don Harris you're thinking of marrying, then who is it?" he finished sceptically.

Ashleigh bit her lip. "It's someone here," she said rashly.

"What? You mean one of the Langtons—the people

who own the station?" Walter demanded, and she nodded. There seemed nothing else to do.

"But it's not official," she murmured uncomfortably. At that instant, she heard a car pull up outside. It would be Charlie, she assured herself after a moment of complete panic because of the lie she'd just told. He must be coming to see if her uncle was ready to go back to the plane. She jumped up hurriedly. "Don't ask me about it now. It—it's all in the air. I'll write and explain—I know you want to get away. . . ."

A car door slammed, firm footsteps sounded, and she turned her head and her blood froze. It wasn't Charlie but Ryan Langton, who was striding purposefully along the verandah. His thick dark hair was ruffled, his boots were dusty, and in spite of his working clothes he looked handsome and virile, and there was an unmistakable air of distinction and authority about him.

He glanced at Walter and then at Ashleigh, whose face was scarlet and whose composure had gone completely to pieces.

"I saw that plane coming in to land and thought I'd better come back to the homestead to see who it was," he said pleasantly, and Ashleigh wished she could disappear through the floor.

"Oh, you needn't have bothered. It's only my uncle, Walter Hewitt," she stammered. "He's just leaving, as a matter of fact. Uncle—this is Ryan Langton." She said the name indistinctly and got to her feet nervously, and hoped desperately that Walter would disappear quietly. But of course she knew he wouldn't.

The two men shook hands cordially, and Ryan asked the inevitable question. "What brings you out here, Mr. Hewitt? I hope you haven't been worried about Ashleigh."

"I'm afraid I have been," Walter said. "She hasn't been in touch with us since she left Perth." He paused

and Ashleigh could practically read his mind. He was
wondering if this was the man she was thinking of
marrying . . . "I came here specifically to take her
home, but she's just been telling me—"

"That everything's fine," Ashleigh put in with an
unnatural-sounding laugh. "You can tell Aunt Esme
that I'm perfectly okay, Uncle. I—I'll drive you out to
the air-strip. . . . It will be all right for me to borrow
one of the cars, won't it?" she asked Ryan, knowing
her colour was high.

"Sure, go right ahead," Ryan agreed sounding slightly puzzled, and Walter said irritably, "I'm not in all that
much of a hurry, Ashleigh. Now I'm here, I want to
satisfy myself about one or two things." He sent Ryan a
penetrating look. "I don't know if you're aware of it,
but my wife and I are completely in the dark about
what's going on. All I know is what Ashleigh's just told
me—that she's romantically involved with someone
here. She's young, and marriage is too serious a
business to go into lightly, as I'm sure you'll agree, and
while I'm here, I'd like to meet the man concerned. Or,
if that's not possible, at least to learn something about
him. He's a member of your family, I believe."

Ashleigh wanted to die on the spot. What on earth
must Ryan think of her? Her legs felt as if they were
about to give way and nothing on earth would have
made her meet his eyes. She longed to be able to say
that Walter had misunderstood, that she hadn't meant
what he thought, but of course that was impossible.

"Yes, of course, I understand," she heard Ryan say
coolly. "And since Ashleigh has chosen to mention the
matter, and my two younger brothers both happen to
be engaged, I must confess to being the lucky man.
Ashleigh and I haven't known each other very long,
and I think she needs a little more time to be sure of
herself. Hence the lack of communication, for which I
must apologise."

Ashleigh could hardly believe her ears. He hadn't given her away! He'd come to her rescue, and she couldn't really think why. She glanced up and found he was smiling at her a little crookedly, his blue eyes quizzical.

"I see." Walter, who had been listening intently turned to Ashleigh. "You like it here, do you?" He paused while she nodded helplessly, then went on thoughtfully, "Well then, I suppose it would be a mistake on my part to insist on your coming back to Perth with me today. Everyone will be happier if you can stay a little longer while you two get to know each other better and make up your minds. I can't see any objections that your aunt could raise. And that," he told Ryan with a wry smile, "is a matter of some importance. . . . There is one other thing though—this car of Don Harris's. I don't want my niece driving it to Darwin. Frankly, I only allowed her to go off on this holiday with the Harrises with great reluctance, and I'd prefer she didn't have any further involvements with Don."

Ryan nodded, and Ashleigh gritted her teeth. Walter just couldn't get it into his head she wasn't a child.

"I'll take care of the car," Ryan said. "I wouldn't have allowed Ashleigh to drive it to Darwin alone in any case."

"You reassure me. I'm grateful. I hope to be seeing more of you, Ryan. You might manage to come down to Perth and visit us in the near future—perhaps when Ashleigh's ready to come home. My wife would like to meet you, I know."

"Thank you. But that of course must depend on Ashleigh," Ryan said, with a sardonic glance in her direction. "Much as I'd like to, I can't make any promises about what the future holds."

Walter laughed confidently. "I'm hopeful. . . . Well, we'll leave it at that." He glanced at his watch. "I'm afraid I'll have to be moving off. I don't want to be flying in the dark."

To Ashleigh's relief, Ryan didn't try to detain him, and they all went out to the car. As they drove out to the air-strip, Ashleigh sitting in the back, she reflected that Ryan had handled the situation very trickily, leaving an opening for her when later she'd have to tell her uncle that there was to be no marriage.

It should have been a relief to say good bye to Walter and see the plane take off, but it wasn't, because now she was alone with Ryan and accountable to him for involving him in her lies. As they started back along the track—and this time she had to sit beside him in the front—she decided to take the initiative and speak first. Actually she hadn't much alternative, because he was saying nothing. She looked at him nervously, wondering what he was thinking, but his profile was uncommunicative and he gave no indication of being aware she was looking at him.

"I'm sorry about that lie," she said after a moment. "I don't want to go back to Perth, and it was the only way I could think of to—to persuade my uncle to let me stay here. He and my aunt have no children of their own and they're inclined to forget I'm an adult and have ideas of my own—that I don't want the same things as they do." She broke off, thinking she was talking about herself too much. "I didn't think you'd ever find out what I'd said."

"Then you haven't learned how difficult it is to keep a secret in the outback," he said raising an eyebrow. "That sort of thing is likely to come out all over the district on the radio telephone. . . . However, it's not bothering me. It's not to my advantage to have you go back to Perth. The ball's in your court now, and you can play it whichever way you like, once I've taken you back to Don Harris."

Ashleigh bit her lip. "Yes, but—you don't have to take me to Darwin. I can manage on my own."

"I daresay you can, but I'm coming with you all the same. Apart from the fact that I promised your uncle something of the sort, it's what I've always intended to do. And you're just going to have to put up with it. You can't have it all your own way, you know."

He said nothing more, but when they reached the homestead he dropped her off and drove away again, and she had the distinct and rather humiliating impression that he'd washed his hands of her. He'd backed up her story, left her a loophole, and now everything was back where it had started. She'd imagined her lie would cause a cyclone, that he'd tear her to shreds, but nothing had happened at all. She wasn't important enough for that. And if he was taking her to Darwin, it was only because it suited him to do so, because Debra was there.

# Chapter Ten

Two days later, they left for Darwin in Don's car. Ashleigh knew Ryan was going to dump her there and let her work her own way out of the lies she'd told, while he settled his unfinished business with Debra. He'd said he had "things to do" in Darwin and she could guess what they were. If nothing else had brought him to his senses, she suspected that the lie she had told had done that.

He wasn't like Don, she discovered during the long hours of driving to Darwin. He had no objections at all to letting her do her share at the wheel while he had a sleep in the back of the car. It was he, however, who did the last stretch into the city. He knew where Nakara was, and that, she reflected gloomily, was because Debra lived there.

It was almost dark when they reached the Carsons' house, half hidden in a garden crowded with tall palms, some of them with flowering orchids attached to their trunks. The gates were open, and Ryan drove in and pulled up. While he took the luggage from the boot, Ashleigh looked nervously up at the house, which was built, as Debra had said, on stilts. She expected someone to come out at the sound of the car, but no one appeared, though Ryan had let Don know that Ashleigh was arriving that evening.

"I'll take your bags up for you in a minute," Ryan said from close behind her. He set her luggage down and took her hands. "Let's say good bye here, before you go inside, Ashleigh."

She felt her fingers clinging to his. Suddenly everything was happening too fast. She couldn't believe he was going to leave her here and disappear from her life forever. Her lips parted in a silent protest, and then he drew her to him and kissed her—gently, yet burningly, so that she was more certain than she'd ever been that she loved him, and less able than ever to accept or believe that he had no deep feelings for her.

"I'll call you up on the phone and see what's happening in a day or so," he murmured, his voice husky.

Ashleigh nodded, but it was little consolation, and she struggled against the tears that had come to her eyes, and were constricting her throat. Unable to speak, she turned away swiftly to climb the long flight of wooden stairs, while Ryan followed with her luggage. The door into the house was open and, scarcely knowing what she was doing, she rang the bell. Her mind was full of Ryan. She wanted the last few minutes back again, she wanted to have said something of what she felt, to have put her arms around him, been close to him for the last time. And that was sheer lunacy. It would have been much more sensible to have told him not to bother phoning her up, because what was the point in keeping a raw wound open?

But it was too late now even to say anything, because someone had come to the door: a middle-aged woman dressed casually in a cool cotton frock and sandals, her hair a little untidy, her face friendly.

"Why, you must be Ashleigh, Don's girl friend! We didn't expect you till much later." Interested dark brown eyes looked her over and then went enquiringly to Ryan. "I'm Joan Hudson, Caryl's mother. Come along in. Don's in the living room. He'll be surprised." Again she glanced at Ryan and Ashleigh introduced him.

"This is Ryan Langton. He had business in Darwin, so he came across in the car with me."

"I won't come in, thanks, Mrs. Hudson," Ryan said easily when they'd shaken hands. He turned to Ashleigh. "Good bye, Ashleigh. Don't forget—I'll be in touch."

Now was her chance to tell him not to bother, but she didn't; she couldn't. "Good bye, Ryan. Thank you for coming with me—and for putting up with me for so long at Crystal Downs." She could hear her voice beginning to break and swallowed hard.

"My pleasure," he said, and, taking her two hands in his, pressed them briefly. Their eyes met and it was all she could do not to fling herself into his arms. She saw his mouth curve in a faint smile; then he let go of her hands and was gone.

"Pleasant man," Joan Hudson murmured. "You were lucky to be looked after by people like that, weren't you?"

Ashleigh nodded, but she wasn't sure whether she was lucky or unlucky. Certainly her life would never be the same again and it was going to take her a long time to recover from what had happened to her heart at Crystal Downs. Blinking back tears, she allowed the other woman to usher her into the house just as Don, using crutches, his shorts revealing one leg encased in plaster, came awkwardly into the hall.

It was strange to see him again and she found she was

looking at him so dispassionately and with such uninvolvement she was shocked.

"Hello, Don," she exclaimed, her voice over-bright. "Your car's here, safe and sound at long last. Ryan came with me, so I didn't get lost or do anything frightful."

"Good." He stood leaning on his crutches and Joan Hudson tactfully disappeared along the hall with one of Ashleigh's suitcases. "It was the least he could do, in my opinion. He certainly took his time arranging for the car to be repaired."

Ashleigh felt herself bristle. "I thought you understood. Charlie—the mechanic—had to go to Port Hedland. His father was dying."

"How about before that?" Don said. "If I'd been there instead of lying in hospital, I'd have gotten things moving."

"I'm sure you would," Ashleigh said stiffly. "But you weren't there and the Langtons had other things to do besides attend to our problems. For which I know I was responsible," she added quickly.

Don shrugged slightly and changed his tactics. "Well, you're here now. Come and I'll show you your room, Leigh. You'll have to carry that bag yourself. I'm hamstrung with these crutches to manipulate, and Joan's just vanished in the direction of the kitchen to finish cooking dinner."

Ashleigh picked up her bag and went along the hall with him. What on earth had ever attracted her to Don, she wondered. The unconventional life he led, perhaps —the fact that it was so different from the way her aunt and uncle expected her to live. And their opposition had only made her admire him more. At any rate, it was all in the past. She knew now quite positively that she could never live with him, or even work with him.

"It's a fair-sized house," he commented, swinging along on his crutches. "But since we were expecting you, Joan's been sleeping in the study. It's lucky for me she's here on holiday. Otherwise I'd have been in the soup, with you not turning up and Caryl and Len taking off on a week-long safari a couple of days ago."

"Oh. How is Caryl managing?" Ashleigh asked, a little uncomfortably.

"Only just," Don said. "She'll be glad you've finally arrived. She was getting a bit sceptical about you, I think."

In the bedroom, a fan whirred quietly in the ceiling and the wooden louvres that formed the wall under the windows had been opened to let in the cool evening air. Ashleigh looked longingly at the bed with its pale green cover. She wished she could have a good sleep instead of having to face the not very pleasant prospect of sorting out her relationship with Don. But it was no use trying to avoid it, because even though he'd never actually asked her to marry him, she knew very well that was what he had in mind. And oddly enough he seemed so sure of himself, so sure of her, which went to show what a besotted little ingenue she must have been.

"I suppose you're tired," he said belatedly. "I'll leave you to change and have a wash. The bathroom's across the hall. Come out to the dining room when you're ready."

Ashleigh nodded and he limped off.

Dinner was not too difficult. Joan Hudson was interested to hear about Crystal Downs, and Ashleigh managed to talk about her sojourn there fairly impersonally, then turned the conversation to the Ord River, where the Hudsons already lived. Afterwards, the two women washed the dishes amicably and then Joan went out to visit friends while Ashleigh joined Don in the sitting room, where he was reading a book on the Kakadu National Park.

"Finished in the kitchen?" he asked, looking up and putting the book aside. "Sit down and we'll have a talk, Leigh. I'm afraid I'm pretty poor company at the moment. This damned plaster cast is giving me hell. I think it must be pressing on a nerve. You might drive me to the hospital tomorrow and I'll get them to do something about it."

"All right," Ashleigh agreed. She dropped down in a chair and looked at him warily, then went on with an effort, "I want to talk to you too, Don. I've been thinking and I'm sorry, but I'm not going to take up your offer to hostess for the tours."

Don's eyes narrowed. "What do you mean? I thought that was all decided long ago, when you were moving heaven and earth to come up here with me. What's put you off the idea?"

"I've changed my mind, that's all," Ashleigh said evenly, though her pulses were hammering.

"Just like that," he said, his face flushing. "At the eleventh hour. . . . You get me into the mess I'm in and then you tell me cheerfully that you're deserting me! What's Caryl going to do? She's pregnant. Have you forgotten that? Len's agreed to stay on till I'm on the mend, but Caryl can't keep it up."

"No, I suppose not," Ashleigh said hardening her heart and determining she wasn't going to be bluffed or bullied into doing something she didn't want to do. "I don't want to sound unreasonable, but Caryl's problems are really nothing to do with me. Besides, it's not as if you couldn't find someone else to take over. There must be plenty of girls looking for work in Darwin."

Don was looking at her intently. "What's happened to you, Leigh? You were keen on the idea before I left you at Crystal Downs. Who's been getting at you?"

"No one," she said shortly. "I told you, I've thought it over and I've changed my mind."

"So what are you going to do? Go back to Perth? I thought you wanted to be independent. I also thought the general idea was that you and I would get married."

Ashleigh bit her lip, remembering what Walter had said—that Don had practically spent her money already. She said flatly, "It wouldn't work, Don."

"Why not?" His hazel eyes looked into hers and she dropped her lashes. "Well?" he insisted.

"There's just not enough feeling between us for that," she said doggedly.

"Rubbish! Marriages have to be built, they're not ready-made. It would work out." He stroked his beard thoughtfully. "I hope you haven't developed a crush on Ryan Langton. You were pretty struck on him when you met him in Broome, weren't you?"

Ashleigh went scarlet. She wanted to deny that she was the least bit interested in Ryan Langton, but somehow she couldn't do it, and she stared at Don wordlessly.

"He's marrying Debra Davis, anyhow," Don went on, taking in her red cheeks. "She called in here yesterday so I know what I'm talking about. . . . I suggest you go to bed and sleep on it, Leigh. It's not as if I were asking you to marry me right away. There's no rush."

"No, but I've done all the thinking I need to do," she said firmly. "I'm sorry it's turned out this way, but there's really nothing more to say."

He was looking at her steadily and she looked back at him. She could see no hurt in his eyes, and when he finally spoke it was merely to say, "You could at least have given yourself a chance to find out if you can take the life here. It's quite different from living on an isolated cattle station. . . . However, if you've made up your mind to run off back to the city, then I suppose that's that. I thought you had more character. I'm disappointed in you, Leigh."

Disappointed. Was that all? she thought wryly. Well, if he really believed that she'd decided she couldn't take the life, she was not going to disillusion him.

"I think I'll go to bed now," she said after a moment. "I'm really tired. Is there anything I can do for you before I go?"

"Not a thing," he said indifferently, and reached for his book. "Good night, Leigh. Thanks for bringing the car across."

"It was the least I could do," she murmured. "Good night, Don."

Tired though she was, she didn't fall asleep for some time. Her thoughts drifted to Ryan, and she knew that if he'd been in a situation similar to Don's, his reaction would have been very different. But that was hardly relevant. He was going to marry Debra, and at this moment they were probably together, planning their marriage. That was something *she'd* have to accept, and acceptance of the inevitable was going to be a lot more difficult for her than it was for Don.

The next day she packed her things again and moved out. Any guilty feelings she might have had about letting Caryl down were completely wiped out when Joan Hudson inadvertently let it drop that the Carsons had taken another girl along on the trip with them, a girl who was eager to take Caryl's place. Obviously, Don must have known that perfectly well, but he'd preferred to keep Ashleigh in the dark.

She drove him to the hospital before she left, waiting while he had his plaster cast made more comfortable and then driving him home again. Ryan hadn't telephoned and she told herself she was glad. She didn't want the pain of hearing from him, of having him ask her politely how things were going, and telling her about his own plans that undoubtedly would include Debra.

She was moving to a hotel right in Darwin, on the waterfront. Joan Hudson had recommended it; if Joan was surprised at what was happening, she kept it to herself and asked no questions. To Ashleigh's relief, Don had made no further efforts to persuade her to change her mind. It was as though he'd taken a ticket in the lottery and was not really surprised that he hadn't drawn a prize. As she waited for her taxi, he mentioned that he was going to look for a partner. "Someone who can run the show while I'm laid up and who has a bit of money to put into it. The more I see of the business, the more obvious it is that it could do with an injection of that kind."

This admission by Don possibly meant that he had been interested in her money, she thought dispassionately.

"What are your plans now, Leigh?" he asked when the taxi pulled up outside the house.

"I'll stay in Darwin a day or two and then I may go back to Perth," she said vaguely, and he nodded.

"I see. It's a pity the tropics have proved too much for you." His smile was not altogether pleasant, and he didn't kiss her good bye. "Your family will be pleased, at all events. . . . When you see Laura, bring her up to date, won't you? I really think she believed you and I were going to make a go of it."

Ashleigh breathed a sigh of relief when she finally escaped.

The hotel was pleasant, not one of the new high-rise buildings that had gone up since the cyclone, but more in the old style, though it had been extensively renovated. The rooms were big and comfortable, and there was an airy lounge with attractive rattan furniture, cool green-and-ivory curtains and cushions, and glass walls looking into a tropical garden. And of course there was a swimming pool.

Having installed herself in her room, she had a light lunch on the patio by the pool, then went out for a look at Darwin. It was a modern city, full of trees, many of which had been planted since the devastation created by Cyclone Tracy, though some of the African mahoganies and the huge old banyans looked as if they'd been there forever. The people in the Smith Street Mall were casual-looking, leisurely, and a fascinating mixture of races, white and black and Asiatic. While it was hot, it wasn't unpleasantly so.

In fact, she decided it was a place where she could live quite happily—if she had work. But her enquiries in that field produced nothing hopeful, and she knew in her heart she'd have to think of going back to Perth. One thing was for sure: she wasn't going to play at work in the mining company. If she was to be employed there, then she was going to be taken seriously. Walter had said they'd talk about her gaining some experience, and she'd hold him to it. Perhaps she'd do a part-time course in accountancy. Why not? She'd been good at mathematics at school. But somehow the idea didn't seem real, and she had the odd feeling that she was encased in a huge glass egg, waiting for it to crack and . . . let the world in? Or let her out?

It was late afternoon when she wandered slowly back to the hotel, wondering how she'd put in the evening, and dreading the thought of going to bed to be tormented by her thoughts and memories.

The telephone rang only minutes after she reached her room. She'd stripped off her clothes and was just about to go to the shower, and she felt her nerves leap with the clamour of the bell.

Somehow she knew, even before she answered, that it was going to be Ryan. He'd said he'd be in touch, and he'd keep his promise. Someone would have told him when he rang the Carsons that she'd moved out, and where. What would she tell him? she wondered, her thoughts a mad confusion. That she'd decided to go back home, to explain to Walter and Esme that her engagement to Ryan Langton hadn't worked out? Meanwhile the sound of his voice—deep, slightly drawling—was making her so weak at the knees that she sank down on the side of the bed.

"Ashleigh?"

"Yes?" she said, her throat tight. "Who is it?" As if she didn't know!

"I'll give you three guesses," he said lightly. "But save them for later."

"What do you mean?" she stammered.

"How soon can you be ready?" he asked, not bothering to answer her.

"Ready for what?" she asked faintly. The conversation wasn't making sense.

"To meet me. I want to talk to you."

"Oh—I—I was just going to take a shower. I've been out. What do you want to talk about?"

He gave a low laugh. "I'm not telling you over the phone. . . . And you'd better hurry up with that shower or I'll be hammering down your door."

Ashleigh thought she must be going out of her mind, but somewhere deep inside she was madly excited. "Where are you?" she asked flusteredly. "At Debra's?"

"No, I'm not at Debra's. I'm right here in the lounge of this hotel. Now are you going to get moving or must I come and fetch you?"

"I'll be right out," she said hastily, and slammed the receiver down. Her heart was thumping and she didn't dare to ask herself what she was hoping for because she knew it was the impossible.

It was probably the quickest shower she'd ever had in her life. It seemed only seconds before she was getting into one of her pretty dresses—the blue-and-violet cotton that was as soft and flowing as silk. She slipped her feet into violet sandals, brushed her hair, and used the merest touch of make-up. Staring into the mirror, she saw a girl with wide brown-velvet eyes, flushed cheeks, and a mouth that trembled slightly. Of course she was insane, imagining he was here for anything but mundane reasons. His conscience was forcing him to see what she was doing. He felt responsible— particularly since he'd met Walter, she thought confusedly. Yet, there'd been that tender note in his voice and she wasn't convinced by a single one of the doubts her muddled reason was trying to thrust upon her. The fact was that he was here in this hotel waiting for her. . . .

He was standing by one of the huge windows when she reached the lounge. A few people were sitting at the low glass-topped tables having pre-dinner drinks, but Ashleigh saw no one except Ryan looking across at her, his eyes vividly blue, the green palms and multicoloured crotons in the garden outside making an exotic background for his dark good looks. As he came towards her, she felt her whole being light up and fly to him.

He stopped within a foot of her, his eyes devouring her from her shining hair to her fragile sandals, while she in turn took in with a feeling of delight that was both emotional and physical his lean muscular figure in Darwin rig of immaculate beige pants and open-necked white shirt. His mouth was curving in a warm smile and his dark hair was just enough ruffled to make her long to run her fingers through it.

"Let's go into the garden," he murmured. He put his arm around her waist and drew her against him as they headed for the tall glass doors across the room.

The garden was empty, and they found a secluded spot scented by frangipani flowers and screened from the windows of the lounge by a wall of yellow bell vine, its big open-mouthed golden flowers glowing in the evening light.

For a long moment they stood and looked at each other, and then he reached out and drew her against him and kissed her long and deeply on the mouth. She kissed him back, hungrily, passionately, with the warm wonderful feeling that she'd come home to where she belonged—here, in this man's arms, with his love around her like a cloak. This was the happy ending that she hadn't believed possible. He wasn't going to marry Debra. He couldn't when he loved her this way—the way she loved him, with tenderness and passion, with a rightness that was incredible.

When his mouth left hers, they looked deeply into each other's eyes, searching, revealing, discovering, without the need for words. Ashleigh heard herself sigh deeply; then as he drew a gentle finger under each of her eyes she smiled at him through her tears.

"I tried to ring you at the Carsons this afternoon to find out what was happening," he said then. "Joan Hudson told me you'd left, booked in at this hotel. That was all she knew and apparently Don didn't feel like coming to the phone to speak to me. I gathered it was all off between you and him. What were you planning to do, Ashleigh? Disappear? Forget everything that had happened between us?"

She bit her lip.

"I didn't think I'd ever see you again," she said slowly. "I thought you were going to marry Debra. Everyone said so."

"I did intend to marry her," he admitted. "We've known each other a long time; we like each other. I used to think of her strictly as a career girl, but lately I'd begun to suspect that she wouldn't be averse to settling down. As I had the same idea, I imagined we could be . . . comfortable together. And then you turned up in Broome and scattered my carefully made plans to the four winds."

"How?" she asked, her heart beating fast.

"Just by looking at me the way you did. I fell as madly in love as if it were for the first time, and I knew I was a fool. You were so young and it seemed sheer lunacy, particularly since Don Harris had already told me and Debra that you were going to marry him."

She shook her head. "That wasn't true. He'd never actually asked me. Though I did have it in mind when we set out from Perth," she added honestly. "But I was beginning to realise that I'd have to get to know him a whole lot better before I rushed into anything."

He made a rueful face. "I thought it was all cut and dried—and I'm not so unprincipled that I can steal another man's girl without giving it a second thought. Anyhow, I reasoned that I was deluding myself, taking a trip back in time. But all the same, I didn't ask Debra to marry me, and I was annoyed with myself for being so irrational. I was annoyed with you too. You seemed intent on stirring me up, and I didn't want to be side-tracked from something I'd made up my mind to. I'd just started to feel I was regaining my senses when you turned up at Crystal Downs. That was the last straw and I tell you I didn't welcome you."

"I was aware of that," she said laughing a little. "I felt terrible."

"And we got deeper and deeper into trouble, didn't we?" he said pulling her to him again. "We couldn't keep away from each other. In next to no time, I knew that what I felt for you wasn't something I could discount. It had nothing to do with nostalgia for the past or anything of that sort, nothing to do with remembering how I'd felt when I was in love with Christine," he added. "I tried to play fair, but I wasn't making a very good fist of it and I felt rotten about the whole business. All I wanted was to get you back to Darwin and it just didn't seem possible."

"Then if Charlie had fixed the car, you'd have let me go—forgotten me," she said, her voice low. It was an unbearable thought and made her shiver, even now with his arms around her.

"No. I planned to go to Darwin with you and fight it out in the open," he said with a slight smile. "In fact, even if you hadn't broken down on Crystal Downs, I think I'd have gone to Darwin—just to see what was happening. I was a really bad case, in fact. And when your uncle turned up and you as good as pushed me into saying I wanted to marry you, it was almost too much. I had a good mind to hold you to it. But I also began to wonder if part of Don's attraction was that your family didn't approve of him, which made you all the more determined to run off with him—the old thing about forbidden fruit. I fully expected to have a battle ahead of me, but it's been a pushover, hasn't it?" He paused to kiss her and to murmur, "You are going to marry me, aren't you, my darling?"

"Yes, of course," she said huskily, lifting her face to his.

Presently they wandered on through the garden, his arm around her waist. The dark was coming fast and the sun looked like a luminous red moon as it floated down towards the sea. It seemed to hover for a few seconds, and then quite suddenly it was gone, leaving the sky a clear, glowing red. It was heavenly to kiss in the scented garden, and when Ashleigh opened her eyes again, it was dark and the first stars were appearing. In a day or two, she thought dreamily, she and Ryan would be flying down to Perth to break the news to Esme and Walter that they were going to be married. She thought of Debra and felt sorry for her, but at least she had her career and her exciting assignment in Bali. For Ashleigh's part, she wanted no more than to marry this man whose arms were around her, to become a true woman of the outback, and to go up in the helicopter some time when they were mustering cattle, she thought with a feeling of excitement. Ryan would let her, she was sure, and Esme need never know. . . .

As they strolled back towards the hotel to celebrate their engagement over dinner, she said on a sigh, "I'm sorry about Debra, Ryan. It doesn't seem fair—"

"Forget it," he said, a little sharply. "She's not a fool. She knew long ago, in Broome, and if she kept hoping, that was her affair. She'll go back to her career. No matter what happens, life goes on. I've hurt her, I know, and I suppose you've hurt Don, but that's how it is with love. Someone gets hurt, and they get over it. I'd have gotten over it if you'd married Don—and you'd have recovered if I'd married Debra."

Never, she thought vehemently. Never in a million years. The lighted windows of the hotel were coming closer, and she pressed her face against his shoulder and felt his arm tighten around her.

Tears came to her eyes as he said softly, "Yes, I'd have gotten over it—but it would have taken me half a lifetime."

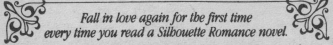

*Fall in love again for the first time
every time you read a Silhouette Romance novel.*

# If you enjoyed this book, and you're ready to be carried away by more tender romance...get 4 romance novels FREE when you become a Silhouette Romance home subscriber.

Act now and we'll send you four touching Silhouette Romance novels. They're our gift to introduce you to our convenient home subscription service. Every month, we'll send you six new Silhouette Romance books. Look them over for 15 days. If you keep them, pay just $11.70 for all six. Or return them at no charge.

We'll mail your books to you two full months *before they are available anywhere else.* Plus, with every shipment, you'll receive the Silhouette Books Newsletter absolutely free. *And Silhouette Romance is delivered free.*

Mail the coupon today to get your four free books—and more romance than you ever bargained for.

Silhouette Romance is a service mark and a registered trademark of Simon & Schuster, Inc.

# Silhouette Romance

## IT'S YOUR OWN SPECIAL TIME
*Contemporary romances for today's women.*
*Each month, six very special love stories will be yours*
*from SILHOUETTE.*

### $1.75 each

| | | | |
|---|---|---|---|
| ☐ 100 Stanford | ☐ 128 Hampson | ☐ 157 Vitek | ☐ 185 Hampson |
| ☐ 101 Hardy | ☐ 129 Converse | ☐ 158 Reynolds | ☐ 186 Howard |
| ☐ 102 Hastings | ☐ 130 Hardy | ☐ 159 Tracy | ☐ 187 Scott |
| ☐ 103 Cork | ☐ 131 Stanford | ☐ 160 Hampson | ☐ 188 Cork |
| ☐ 104 Vitek | ☐ 132 Wisdom | ☐ 161 Trent | ☐ 189 Stephens |
| ☐ 105 Eden | ☐ 133 Rowe | ☐ 162 Ashby | ☐ 190 Hampson |
| ☐ 106 Dailey | ☐ 134 Charles | ☐ 163 Roberts | ☐ 191 Browning |
| ☐ 107 Bright | ☐ 135 Logan | ☐ 164 Browning | ☐ 192 John |
| ☐ 108 Hampson | ☐ 136 Hampson | ☐ 165 Young | ☐ 193 Trent |
| ☐ 109 Vernon | ☐ 137 Hunter | ☐ 166 Wisdom | ☐ 194 Barry |
| ☐ 110 Trent | ☐ 138 Wilson | ☐ 167 Hunter | ☐ 195 Dailey |
| ☐ 111 South | ☐ 139 Vitek | ☐ 168 Carr | ☐ 196 Hampson |
| ☐ 112 Stanford | ☐ 140 Erskine | ☐ 169 Scott | ☐ 197 Summers |
| ☐ 113 Browning | ☐ 142 Browning | ☐ 170 Ripy | ☐ 198 Hunter |
| ☐ 114 Michaels | ☐ 143 Roberts | ☐ 171 Hill | ☐ 199 Roberts |
| ☐ 115 John | ☐ 144 Goforth | ☐ 172 Browning | ☐ 200 Lloyd |
| ☐ 116 Lindley | ☐ 145 Hope | ☐ 173 Camp | ☐ 201 Starr |
| ☐ 117 Scott | ☐ 146 Michaels | ☐ 174 Sinclair | ☐ 202 Hampson |
| ☐ 118 Dailey | ☐ 147 Hampson | ☐ 175 Jarrett | ☐ 203 Browning |
| ☐ 119 Hampson | ☐ 148 Cork | ☐ 176 Vitek | ☐ 204 Carroll |
| ☐ 120 Carroll | ☐ 149 Saunders | ☐ 177 Dailey | ☐ 205 Maxam |
| ☐ 121 Langan | ☐ 150 Major | ☐ 178 Hampson | ☐ 206 Manning |
| ☐ 122 Scofield | ☐ 151 Hampson | ☐ 179 Beckman | ☐ 207 Windham |
| ☐ 123 Sinclair | ☐ 152 Halston | ☐ 180 Roberts | ☐ 208 Halston |
| ☐ 124 Beckman | ☐ 153 Dailey | ☐ 181 Terrill | ☐ 209 LaDame |
| ☐ 125 Bright | ☐ 154 Beckman | ☐ 182 Clay | ☐ 210 Eden |
| ☐ 126 St. George | ☐ 155 Hampson | ☐ 183 Stanley | ☐ 211 Walters |
| ☐ 127 Roberts | ☐ 156 Sawyer | ☐ 184 Hardy | ☐ 212 Young |

### $1.95 each

| | | | |
|---|---|---|---|
| ☐ 213 Dailey | ☐ 217 Vitek | ☐ 221 Browning | ☐ 225 St. George |
| ☐ 214 Hampson | ☐ 218 Hunter | ☐ 222 Carroll | ☐ 226 Hampson |
| ☐ 215 Roberts | ☐ 219 Cork | ☐ 223 Summers | ☐ 227 Beckman |
| ☐ 216 Saunders | ☐ 220 Hampson | ☐ 224 Langan | ☐ 228 King |

## Silhouette Romance

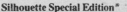